"Should you [...] position on [...] you would be well paid even though there is no work involved."

"No work involved?"

Darcy was soothed to receive the exact response she had anticipated in that interruption. "No work whatsoever," she confirmed. "While you were living in my home, your time would be your own, and at the end of your employment—assuming that you fulfill the terms to my satisfaction—I would also give you a very generous bonus."

"What's the catch?" Luca prompted very softly. "In return you ask me to do something illegal?"

A mortified flush stained Darcy's perfect skin. "Of course not," she rebutted tautly. "The 'catch', if you choose to call it that, is that you would have to marry me for six months!"

Dear Reader,

What I enjoy most about writing is the creation of entirely different heroines. THE HUSBAND HUNTERS is about three women who find love where they least expect it. Maxie cannot imagine any man appreciating her for herself, rather than her looks. Darcy had been badly hurt and has given up on the male sex. Polly falls in love and is betrayed. To match these ladies, we have Angelos, who fondly imagines that Maxie will be his the instant he asks; Luca, who seeks revenge by ensuring that Darcy marries no one but him; and Raul, who finds out the hard way that Polly, the idealistic mother of his child, can be surprisingly unforgiving....

Sincerely

*Lynne Graham*

Look out next month for Polly's story:
**Contract Baby** by Lynne Graham
Harlequin Presents #2013

# LYNNE GRAHAM

## The Vengeful Husband

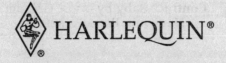

HARLEQUIN®

TORONTO • NEW YORK • LONDON
AMSTERDAM • PARIS • SYDNEY • HAMBURG
STOCKHOLM • ATHENS • TOKYO • MILAN • MADRID
PRAGUE • WARSAW • BUDAPEST • AUCKLAND

ISBN 0-373-12007-9

THE VENGEFUL HUSBAND

First North American Publication 1999.

Copyright © 1998 by Lynne Graham.

**Printed in U.S.A.**

# CHAPTER ONE

A SLENDER fragile beauty in a silvery green gown. Translucent skin, a mane of vibrant Titian hair and spellbinding eyes as green as peridots behind her flirtatious little mask. A hoarse, sexy little voice, sharp enough to strip paint and then sweet enough to make honey taste bitter...

'No names...no pack drill,' she had said.

'I don't want to know,' she had said, when he had tried to identify himself. 'After tonight, I'll never see you again. What would be the point?'

No woman had ever said that to Gianluca Raffacani before. No woman had ever looked on him as a one-night stand. The shock of such treatment had been profound. But her eagerness in his bed had seemed to disprove the dismissive words on her lips...until he'd wakened in the early hours and found his mystery lover gone and the Adorata ring gone with her. And then Luca had simply not been able to credit that some unscrupulous little tart had contrived to rip him off with such insulting ease.

His memory of that disastrous night in Venice almost three years earlier still biting like salt in an open wound, Luca surveyed the closed file labelled 'Darcy Fielding' on his library desk, his chiselled features chillingly cast. With the cool of a self-discipline renowned in the world of international finance, he resisted the temptation to rip open the file like an impatient boy. He had waited a long time for this moment. He could wait a little longer. 'It is *her* this time...you're sure?' he prompted softly.

Even swollen with pride as Benito was at finally succeeding in his search, even convinced by the facts that he had to have the right woman, Benito still found himself

5

stiffening with uncertainty. Although the woman he had identified matched every slender clue he had started out with, by no stretch of his imagination could he see his famously fastidious and highly sophisticated employer choosing to spend a wild night of passion with the female in that photograph...

'I will only be sure when you have recognised her, sir,' Benito admitted tautly.

'You're backtracking, Benito.' With a rueful sigh that signified no great hope of satisfaction, Luca Raffacani reached out a deceptively indolent brown hand and flipped open the file to study the picture of the woman on the title page.

As Luca tensed and a frown grew on his strong dark face, setting his pure bone structure to the cold consistency of granite, Benito paled, suddenly convinced that he had made a complete ass of himself. That bedraggled female image sported worn jeans, wellington boots, a battered rain-hat and a muddy jacket with a long rip in one sleeve. More bag lady than gorgeous seductress. 'I've been too hasty—'

'She's cut off her hair...' his employer interrupted in a low-pitched growl.

After a convulsive swallow, Benito breathed tautly, 'Are you saying that...it *is* the same woman?'

'Was she got up like this for a fancy dress party?'

'Signorina Fielding was feeding hens when that was taken,' Benito supplied apologetically. 'It was the best the photographer could manage. She doesn't go out much.'

'Hens...?' Bemusement pleating his aristocratic ebony brows, Luca continued to scan the photo with hard, dark deepset eyes. 'Yet it is her. Without a doubt, it is her...the devious little thief who turned me over like a professional!'

Darcy Fielding had stolen a medieval ring, a museum piece, an irreplaceable heirloom. The Raffacani family had been princes since the Middle Ages. To mark the occasion of the birth of his son, the very first *principe* had given his wife, Adorata, the magnificent ruby ring. Yet in spite of that rich family heritage, and the considerable value of the jewel, the police had not been informed of the theft. Initially stunned by such an omission, Benito had since become less surprised...

According to popular report within the Raffacani empire, some very strange things had happened the night of the annual masked ball at the Palazzo d'Oro. The host had vanished, for one thing. And if it was actually true that Gianluca Raffacani had vanished in order to romance the thief with something as deeply uncool for a native Venetian as a moonlit gondola tour of the city, Benito could perfectly understand why the police had been excluded from the distinctly embarrassing repercussions of that evening. No male would wish to confess to such a cardinal error of judgement.

In spite of the substantial reward which had been dangled like bait in the relevant quarters, the ring had not been seen since. Most probably it had been disposed of in England— secretly acquired by some rich collector content not to question its provenance. Benito had been extremely disappointed when the investigator failed to turn up the slightest evidence of Darcy Fielding having a previous criminal record.

'Tell me about her...' his employer invited without warning, shutting the file with a decisive snap and thrusting it aside.

Surprised by the instruction, Benito breathed in deep. 'Darcy Fielding lives in a huge old house which has been in her family for many generations. Her financial situation is dire. The house is heavily mortgaged and she is currently behind with the repayments—'

'Who holds the mortgage?' Luca incised softly.

Benito informed him that the mortgage had been taken out a decade earlier with an insurance firm.

'Buy it,' Luca told him equally quietly. 'Continue...'

'Locally, the lady is well-respected. However, when the

investigator went further afield, he found her late god-mother's housekeeper more than willing to dish the dirt.'

Luca's brilliant eyes narrowed, his sensual mouth twisting with distaste. In an abrupt movement, he reopened the file at the photograph again. He surveyed it with renewed fascination. What he could see of her hair suggested a brutal shearing rather than the attentions of a salon. She looked a mess, a total mess, but the glow of that perfect skin and the bewitching clarity of those eyes were unmistakable.

Emerging from his uncharacteristic loss of attention, Luca discovered that he had also lost the thread of Benito's report...

'And if the lady pulls it off, she stands to inherit something in the region of one million pounds sterling,' Benito concluded impressively.

Luca studied his most trusted aide. 'Pull what off?'

'The late Signora Leeward had three god-daughters...possibly the god-daughters from hell.' Benito labelled them with rueful amusement. 'When it came to the disposing of her worldly goods, what was there to choose between the three? One living with a married man, one an unmarried mother and the other going the same way—and not a wedding ring or even the prospect of one between the lot of them!'

'You've lost me,' Luca admitted with controlled impatience.

'Darcy Fielding's rich godmother left everything to her three godchildren on condition that each of them find a husband within the year.'

'And Darcy is one of those women you described.' Luca finally grasped it, bronzed features freezing into charged stillness. *'Which?'*

'She's the unmarried mother,' Benito volunteered.

Luca froze. 'When was the child born?'

'Seven months after her trip to Venice. The kid's just over two.'

Luca stared into space, rigidly schooling his dark face to

impassivity, but it was a challenge to suppress his sheer outrage at the news. *Cristo*...she had even been pregnant with another man's child when she slept with him! Well, that was just one more nail in her coffin. Luca swore in disgust. Whatever was most important to her, he would take from her in punishment. He would teach her what it was like to be deceived and cheated and humiliated. As *she,* most unforgettably, had taught *him*...

'As to the identity of the kid's father...' Benito continued wryly. 'The jury's still out on that one. Apparently the locals believe that the child was fathered by the fiancé, who ditched the lady at the altar. He figures as a rat of the lowest order in their eyes. But the godmother's housekeeper had a very different version of events. *She* contends that the fiancé was abroad at the time the kid was conceived, and that he took to his heels because he realised that the baby on the way couldn't possibly be his!'

Luca absorbed that further information in even stonier silence.

'I shouldn't think the lady will remain a single parent for long,' Benito advanced with conviction. 'Not with a million pounds up for grabs. And on page six of the file you will see what I believe she is doing to acquire that money...'

Luca leafed through the file. 'What is this?' he demanded, studying the tiny print of the enclosed newspaper advertisement and its accompanying box number.

'I suspect that Darcy Fielding is discreetly advertising for a husband to fulfil the terms of that will.'

'*Advertising?*' Luca echoed in raw disbelief.

*Country woman seeks quiet, well-behaved and domesticated single male without close ties, 25-50, for short-term live-in employment. Absolute confidentiality guaranteed. No time-wasters, please.*

'That's not an advertisement for a husband...it's an ad for an emasculated household pet!' Luca launched with incredulous bite.

'I'm going to have to advertise again,' Darcy divulged grimly to Karen as she mucked out the stall of the single elderly occupant in the vast and otherwise horse-free stable yard. She wielded the shovel like an aggressive weapon. Back to square one. She could hardly believe it—and that wretched advertisement had cost an arm and a leg!

Standing by and willing to help, but knowing better than to offer, Karen looked in surprise at her friend. 'But what happened to your shortlist of two possibilities? The gardener and the home handyman?'

Darcy slung the attractive thirty-year-old brunette a weary grimace. 'Yesterday I phoned one and then the other in an attempt to set up an interview—'

'In which you planned to finally spill the confidential beans that matrimony was the *real* employment on offer.' Karen sighed. 'Boy, would I like to have been a fly on the wall when you broke that news!'

'Yes, well...as it turns out, I shan't need to embarrass myself just yet. One had already found a job elsewhere and the other has moved on without leaving a forwarding address. I shouldn't have wasted so much time agonising over my choice.'

'*What* choice? You only got five replies. Two were obscene and one was weird! The ad was too vague in one way and far too specific in the other. What on earth possessed you to put in "well-behaved and domesticated"? I mean, talk about picky, why don't you? Still, I can't really say I'm sorry that you've drawn a blank,' Karen admitted, with the bluntness that made the two women such firm friends.

'Karen...' Darcy groaned.

'Look, the thought of you being alone in this house with some stranger gives me the shivers!' the brunette confided anxiously. 'In any case, since you didn't want to risk admitting in the ad that you were actually looking for a temporary husband, what are the chances that either of those men would have been agreeable to the arrangement you were about to offer?'

Darcy straightened in frustration. 'If I'd offered enough money, I bet one of them would have agreed. I *need* my inheritance, Karen. I don't care what I have to do to get it. I don't care if I have to marry the Hunchback of Notre Dame to meet the conditions of Nancy's will!' Darcy admitted with driven honesty. 'This house has been in my family for four *hundred* years—'

'But it's crumbling round your ears and eating you up alive, Darcy. Your father had no right to lay such a burden on you. If he hadn't let Fielding's Folly get in such a state while *he* was responsible for it, you wouldn't be facing the half of what you're facing right now!'

Darcy tilted her chin, green eyes alight with stubborn determination. 'Karen…as long as I have breath in my body and two hands to work with, the Folly will survive so that I can pass it on to Zia.'

Pausing to catch her breath from her arduous labour, Darcy glanced at her two-year-old daughter. Seated in a grassy sunlit corner, Zia was grooming one of her dolls with immense care. Her watching mother's gaze was awash with wondering pride and pleasure.

Zia had been blessed at birth, Darcy conceded gratefully. Mercifully, she hadn't inherited her mother's carroty hair, myopic eyesight *or* her nose. Zia had lustrous black curls and dainty, even features. There was nothing undersized or over-thin about her either. She was a strikingly pretty and feminine little girl. In short, she was already showing all the promise of becoming everything her mother had once so painfully and pointlessly longed to be…

Zia wouldn't be a wallflower at parties, too blunt-spoken to be flirtatious or appealing, too physically plain to attract attention any other way. Nor would Zia ever be so full of self-pity that she threw herself into the bed of a complete stranger just to prove that she *could* attract a man. Pierced to the heart by that painful memory, Darcy paled and guiltily looked away from her child, wondering how the heck she would eventually explain that shameful reality in terms that wouldn't hurt and alienate her daughter.

Some day Zia would ask her father's name, quite reasonably, perfectly understandably. And what did Darcy have to tell her? Oh, I never got his name because I told him I didn't want it. Even worse, I could well walk past him on the street without recognising him, because I wasn't wearing my contacts and I'm a little vague as to his actual features. But he had dark eyes, even darker hair, and a wonderful, wonderful voice...

Beneath Karen's frowning gaze, Darcy had turned a beet-root colour and had begun studiously studying her booted feet. 'What's up?'

'Indigestion,' Darcy muttered flatly, and it wasn't a lie. Memories of that nature made her feel queasy and crushed her self-respect flat. She had been a push-over for the first sweet-talking playboy she had ever met.

'So it's back to the drawing board as far as the search for a temporary hubby goes, I gather...' Releasing her breath in a rueful hiss, Karen studied the younger woman and reluctantly dug an envelope from the pocket of her jeans and extended it. 'Here, take it. A late applicant, I assume. It came this morning. The postmark's a London one.'

To protect Darcy's anonymity, Karen had agreed to put her own name behind the advertisement's box number. All the replies had been sent to the gate lodge which Karen had recently bought from the estate. Darcy was well aware that she was running a risk in advertising to find a husband, but no other prospect had offered. If she was found out, she could be accused of trying to circumvent the conditions of her godmother's will and excluded from inheriting. But what else was she supposed to do? Darcy asked herself in guilty desperation.

It was *her* duty and *her* responsibility alone to secure Fielding's Folly for future generations. She could not fail the trust her father had imposed on her at the last. She had faithfully promised that no matter what the cost she would hold on to the Folly. How could she allow four hundred years of family history to slip through her careless fingers?

And, even more importantly, only when she contrived to marry would she be in a position to re-employ the estate staff forced to seek work elsewhere after her father's death. In the months since, few had found new jobs. The knowledge that such loyal and committed people were still suffering from her father's financial incompetence weighed even more heavily on her conscience.

Tearing the envelope open, Darcy eagerly scanned the brief letter and her bowed shoulders lifted even as she read. 'He's not of British birth...and he has experience as a financial advisor—'

'Probably once worked as a bank clerk,' Karen slotted in, cynically unimpressed by the claim. A childless divorcee, Karen was comfortably off but had little faith in the reliability of the male sex.

'He's offering references upfront, which is more than anyone else did.' Darcy's state of desperation was betrayed by the optimistic look already blossoming in her expressive eyes. '*And* he's only thirty-one.'

'What nationality?'

In the act of frowning down at the totally illegible signature, Darcy raised her head again. 'He doesn't say. He just states that he is healthy and single and that a temporary position with accommodation included would suit him right now—'

'So he's unemployed and broke.'

'If he wasn't unemployed and willing to move in, he wouldn't be applying, Karen,' Darcy pointed out gently. 'It's a reasonable letter. Since he didn't know what the job

was, he's sensibly confined himself to giving basic information only.'

As she paced the confines of Karen's tiny front room in the
gate lodge five days later, Darcy pushed her thick-lensed
spectacles up the bridge of her nose, smoothed her hands
down over her pleated skirt and twitched at the roll collar
of her cotton sweater as if it was choking her.

*He* would be here in five minutes. And she hadn't even
managed to speak to the guy yet! Since he hadn't given her
a phone number to contact him, she had had to write back
to his London address and, nervous of giving out her own
phone number at this stage, she had simply set up an interview and asked him to let her know if the date didn't
suit. He had sent a brief note of confirmation, from which
she had finally divined that his christian name appeared to
be a surprisingly English-sounding Lucas, but as for his
surname, she would defy a handwriting expert to read that
swirling scrawl!

Hearing the roar of a motorbike out on the road, Darcy
suppressed her impatience. Lucas was late. Maybe he
wasn't going to show. But a minute later the door burst
open. Karen poked her head in, her face filled with excitement. 'A monster motorbike just drew up…and this absolutely edible hunk of male perfection took off his helmet!
It has to be Lucas…and Darcy, he is *gorgeous*—'

'He's come on a motorbike?' Darcy interrupted with a
look of astonishment.

'You are *so* stuffy sometimes,' Karen censured. 'And I
bet you a fiver you can't work up the nerve to ask this
particular bloke if he'd be prepared to marry you for a fee!'

Darcy was already painfully aware that she had no choice
whatsoever on that count. She *had* to ask. She was praying
that Lucas, whoever he was and whatever he was like,
would agree. She didn't have the time to readvertise. Her
back was up against the wall. Yesterday she had received
a letter from the company that held the mortgage on

Fielding's Folly. They were threatening to repossess the house and, since she already had a big overdraft, the bank would not help without a guarantee that she would in the near future have the funds to settle her obligations.

Darcy winced as the doorbell shrilled. Karen bolted to answer it. Bolted—yes, that was the only possible word for her friend's indecent eagerness to reach the front door. Face wooden and set, Darcy positioned herself by the fireplace. So he was attractive. Attractive men had huge egos. She grimaced. All she wanted was someone ordinary and unobtrusive, but what she wanted she wouldn't necessarily get.

'Signorina Darcy?' she heard an accented drawl question in a tone of what sounded like polite surprise.

'No…she's, er, through here…er, waiting for you,' Karen stammered with a dismayingly girlish giggle, and the lounge door was thrust wide.

Blinking rapidly, Darcy was already glued to the spot, a deep frown-line bisecting her brow. That beautiful voice had struck such an eerie chord of familiarity she was transfixed, heart beating so fast she was convinced it might burst. And then mercifully she understood the source of that strange familiarity and shivered, thoroughly spooked. Dear heaven, he was Italian! It was that lyrical accent she had recognised, *not* the voice.

A very tall, dark male, sporting sunglasses and sheathed in motorbike leathers, strode into the small room. Involuntarily Darcy simply gaped at him, her every expectation shattered. Black leather accentuated impossibly wide shoulders, narrow hips and long, lean powerful thighs. Indeed the fidelity of fit left little of that overpoweringly masculine physique to the imagination. And the sunglasses lent his dark features an intimidating lack of expression. And yet…and *yet* as Darcy surveyed him with startled eyes she realised that he shared more than an accent with Zia's father. He had also been very tall and well-built.

So what? an irritated voice screeched through her blitzed

brain. So you're meeting *another* tall, dark Italian…big deal! The silver-tongued sophisticate who had got her pregnant wouldn't have been caught dead in such clothing. And if she hadn't had such a guilt complex about her wanton behaviour in Venice, she wouldn't be feeling this incredibly foolish sense of threatening familiarity, she told herself in complete exasperation.

'Please excuse me for continuing to wear my sunglasses. I have been suffering from eye strain…the light, it hurts my eyes,' he informed her in a deep, dark drawl that was both well-modulated and unexpectedly quiet.

'Won't you sit down?' Darcy invited, with an uncharacteristically weak motion of one hand as she forced herself almost clumsily down into a seat.

But then Darcy was in shock. She had hoped he would be either sensible and serious or weak and biddable. Instead she had been presented with a rampantly macho male who roared up on a motorbike and wore trousers so tight she marvelled that he could stand in them, never mind sit down. With what she believed was termed designer stubble on his aggressive jawline, he looked about as domesticated and well-behaved as a sabre-toothed tiger.

'If you will forgive me for saying so…you look at me rather strangely,' he remarked, further disconcerting her as he lowered himself down with indolent grace onto the small sofa opposite her. 'Do I remind you of someone, *signorina?*'

Darcy stiffened even more with nervous tension, and she was already sitting rigid-backed in the seat. 'Not at all,' she asserted with deflating conviction. 'Now, since I'm afraid I couldn't read your signature…what is your full name?'

'Let us leave it at Luca for now. The wording of your ad suggested that the employment on offer could be of a somewhat unusual nature,' he drawled softly. 'I would like some details before we go any further.'

Darcy bristled like a cat stroked the wrong way. She was supposed to be interviewing him, not the other way round!

'After all, you have not given me your real name either,' he pointed out in offensively smooth continuance.

Darcy's eyes opened to their fullest extent. 'I beg your pardon?'

'Before I came down here, I checked you out. Your surname is Fielding, *not* Darcy, and you do *not* live here in this cottage; you live in the huge mansion at the top of the driveway,' he enumerated with unabashed cool. 'You have gone to some trouble to conceal your own identity. Naturally that is a source of concern to me.'

Stunned by that little speech, Darcy sprang upright and stared down at him in shaken disbelief, her angry bewilderment unconcealed. '*You* checked *me* out?'

He lifted a casual brown hand and slowly removed the sunglasses. 'The light is dim enough in here...'

He studied her with a curiously expectant quality of intensity.

And without warning Darcy found herself staring down into lustrous dark eyes fringed by glossy, spiky black lashes. He had the sort of eyes that packed a powerful punch. Gorgeous, she thought in helpless reaction, brilliant and dark as night, impenetrably deep and unreadable. With the sunglasses on he had looked as if he might be pretty good-looking, without them he zoomed up the scale to stunningly handsome, in spite of the fact that he badly needed a shave. And she now quite understood that hint of expectancy he betrayed. This was a guy accustomed to basking in female double takes, appreciative stares and inviting smiles.

But Darcy tensed and took an instantaneous step back, her retreat only halted by the armchair she had vacated. Yet the tiny twisting sensation of sudden excitement she had experienced still curled up deep in the pit of her taut stomach, and then pierced her like a knife with sudden shame. Her colour heightening, Darcy plotted her path out of the way of the armchair behind her, controlled solely by a need to put as much distance as possible between them.

Throughout that unchoreographed backing away process of hers, she was tracked by narrowed unflinchingly steady dark eyes. 'Signorina Fielding—'

'Look, you had no right to check me out…' Darcy folded her arms in a defensive movement. 'I guaranteed your privacy. Couldn't you have respected mine?'

'Not without some idea of what I might be getting into. It's standard business practice to make enquiries in advance of an interview.'

Darcy tore her frustrated gaze from his. Antipathy darted through her in a blinding wave. With difficulty, she held onto her ready temper. Possibly the reminder had been a timely one. It was, after all, a business proposition she intended to make. And this Luca might think he was clever, but she already knew he had to be as thick as two short planks, didn't she? Only a complete idiot would turn up for an interview with a woman unshaven and dressed like a Hell's Angel. A financial advisor? In his dreams! Conservative apparel went with such employment.

Bolstered by the belief that he could be no Einstein, and rebuking herself for having been intimidated by something as superficial and unimportant as his physical appearance, Darcy sat down again and linked her small hands tightly together on her lap. 'Right, let's get down to business, then…'

The waiting silence lay thick and heavy like a blanket. Settling back into the sofa in a relaxed sprawl of long, seemingly endless limbs, Luca surveyed her with unutterable tranquillity.

Her teeth gritted. Wondering just how long that laid-back attitude would last, Darcy lifted her chin to a challenging angle. 'There *was* a good reason behind the offbeat ad I placed. But before I explain what that reason is, I should mention certain facts in advance. Should you agree to take the position on offer, you would be well paid even though there is no work involved—'

'*No* work involved?'

Darcy was soothed at receiving the exact response she had anticipated in that interruption. 'No work whatsoever,' she confirmed. 'While you were living in my home, your time would be your own, and at the end of your employment—assuming that you fulfil the terms to my satisfaction—I would also give you a generous bonus.'

'So what's the catch?' Luca prompted very softly. 'In return you ask me to do something illegal?'

A mortified flush stained Darcy's perfect skin. 'Of course not,' she rebutted tautly. 'The "catch", if you choose to call it that, is that you would have to agree to marry me for six months!'

'To...*marry* you?' Luca stressed the word with a frown of wondering incredulity as he sat forward on the sofa. 'The employment you offer is...*marriage?*'

'Yes. It's really quite simple. I need a man to go through a wedding ceremony with me and behave like a husband for a minimum of six months,' Darcy extended, with the frozen aspect of a woman forcing herself to refer to an indecent act.

'Why?'

'Why? That's my business. I don't think you require that information to make a decision,' Darcy responded uncomfortably.

Lush black lashes semi-screened his dark eyes. 'I don't understand... Could you explain it again, *signorina,*' he urged, in a rather dazed undertone.

You certainly couldn't call him mentally agile, Darcy thought ruefully. Having got over the worst, however, she felt stronger, and all embarrassment had left her. He was still sitting there, and why shouldn't he be? If he was as single as he had said he was, he stood to earn a great deal for doing nothing. She repeated what she had already said and, convinced that the financial aspect would be the greatest persuader of all, she mentioned the monthly salary she was prepared to offer and then the sizeable bonus she would advance in return for his continuing discretion about their arrangement after they had parted.

He nodded, and then nodded again more slowly, still focusing with a slight frown on the worn carpet at his feet. Maybe the light was annoying his eyes, Darcy decided, struggling to hold onto her irritation at his torpid reactions. Maybe he was just gobsmacked by the concept of being paid to be bone idle. Or maybe he was so shattered by what she had suggested that he hadn't yet worked out how to respond.

'I would, of course, require references,' Darcy continued.

'I could not supply references as a husband...'

Darcy drew in a deep breath of restraint. 'I'm referring to character references,' she said drily.

'If you wanted a husband, why didn't you place an ad in the personal column?'

'I would have received replies from men interested in a genuine and lasting marriage.' Darcy sighed. 'It was wiser just to advertise my requirements as a form of employment—'

'Quiet...domesticated...well-behaved.'

'I don't want someone who's going to get under my feet or expect me to wait on him hand and foot. Would you say you were self-sufficient?'

'*Si...*'

'Well, then, what do you think?' Darcy demanded impulsively.

'I don't yet know what I think. I wasn't expecting this kind of proposal,' he returned gently. 'No woman has ever asked me to marry her before.'

'I'm not talking about a proper marriage. Obviously we'd separate after the six months was up and get a divorce. By the way, you would also have to sign a pre-nuptial contract,' Darcy added, because she needed to safeguard the estate from any claim an estranged husband might legitimately attempt to make. 'That isn't negotiable.'

Luca rose gracefully upright. 'I believe I would need a greater cash inducement to give up my freedom—'

'That's not a problem,' Darcy broke in, her tone one of eager reassurance on that point. If he was prepared to consider her proposition, she was keen to accommodate him. 'I'm prepared to negotiate. If you agree, I'll double the original bonus I offered.'

Disconcertingly, he didn't react to that impulsive offer. Darcy flushed then, feeling more than a little foolish.

Veiled dark eyes surveyed her. 'I'll think it over. I'll be in touch.'

'The references?'

'I will present them if I decide to accept the…the position.' As Luca framed the last two words a flash of shimmering gold illuminated his dark eyes. Amusement at the sheer desperation she had revealed in her desire to reach agreement with him? Darcy squirmed at the suspicion.

'I need an answer very soon. I have no time to waste.'

'I'll give you an answer tomorrow…' He strode to the door and then he hesitated, throwing her a questioning look over one broad masculine shoulder. 'It surprises me that you could not persuade a friend to agree to so temporary an arrangement.'

Darcy stiffened and coloured. 'In these particular circumstances, I prefer a stranger.'

'A stranger…I can understand that,' Luca completed in a honey-soft and smooth drawl.

# CHAPTER TWO

'So what sort of impression did Lucas make on you?' Karen demanded, minutes later.

'It's not Lucas, it's Luca... My impression?' Darcy studied her friend with a frowning air of abstraction. 'That's the odd thing. I didn't really get a proper impression—at least not one I could hang onto for longer than five seconds,' she found herself admitting in belated recognition of the fact. 'One minute I thought he was all brawn and no brain, and then the next he would come out with something razor-sharp. And towards the end he was as informative as a brick wall.'

'He didn't accuse you of dragging him down here on false pretences? He didn't laugh like a drain? Or even ask if you were pulling his leg?' It was Karen's turn to look confused.

Darcy shook her head reflectively. 'He was very low-key in his reactions, businesslike in spite of the way he was dressed. That made it easier for me. I didn't get half as embarrassed as I thought I would.'

'Only you could conduct such a weird and loaded interview with a male that gorgeous and not respond on any more personal a level.'

'That kind of man leaves me cold.' But Darcy's cheeks warmed as she recalled that humiliating moment when she had reacted all too personally to the sheer male magnetism of those dark good looks.

Karen's keen gaze gleamed. 'He *didn't* leave you stone-cold...did he?'

Cursing her betrayingly fair skin, Darcy strove to continue meeting her friend's eyes levelly. 'Karen—'

'Forget it… I can tell a mile off when you're about to lie through your teeth!'

Darcy winced. 'OK…I noticed that Luca was reasonably fanciable—'

'*Reasonably fanciable?*' her friend carolled with extravagant incredulity.

'All right.' Darcy sighed in rueful surrender. 'He was spectacular…are you satisfied now?'

'Yes. Your indifference to men seriously worries me. Now at least I know that you're still in the land of the living.'

Darcy pulled a wry face. 'With my level of looks and appeal, indifference is by far the safest bet, believe me.'

Karen compressed her lips and thought with real loathing of all the people responsible for ensuring Darcy had such a low opinion of her own attractions. Her cold and critical father, her vain and sarcastic stepmother, not to mention the rejections her unlucky friend had suffered from the opposite sex during her awkward and vulnerable teen years. Being jilted at the altar and left to raise her child alone had completed the damage.

And these days Darcy dressed like a scarecrow and made little effort to socialise. Slowly and surely she was turning into a recluse, although the hours she slaved over that wretched house meant that she didn't know what free time was, Karen conceded grimly. Anyone else confronted with such an immense and thankless challenge would've given up and at least sold the furniture by now, but not Darcy. Darcy would starve sooner than see any more of the Folly's treasures go to auction.

'I get really annoyed with you when you talk like that,' Karen said truthfully. 'If you would only buy some decent clothes and take a little more interest in—'

'Why bother when I'm quite happy as I am?' Visibly agitated by the turn the conversation had taken, Darcy glanced hurriedly at her watch and added with a relief she couldn't hide, 'It's time I picked up Zia from the play-group.'

As Darcy left the gate lodge, however, that final dialogue travelled with her. Demeaning memories had been roused to fill her thoughts and unsettle her stomach. All over again she saw her one-time fiancé, Richard, gawping at her chief bridesmaid like a moonsick calf and finally admitting at the eleventh hour that he couldn't go through with the wedding because he had fallen in love with Maxie. And the ultimate insult had to be that her former friend, Maxie, who was so beautiful she could stop traffic, hadn't even *wanted* Richard!

That devastatingly public rejection had been followed by the Venetian episode, Darcy recalled wretchedly. That, too, had ended in severe humiliation. She had got to play Cinderella for a night. And then she had got to stand on the Ponte della Guerra and be stood up like a dumb teenager the following day. She had waited for ages too, and had hit complete rock-bottom when she finally appreciated that Prince Charming was not going to turn up.

Of course another woman, a more experienced and less credulous woman, would have known that that so casually voiced yet so romantic suggestion had been the equivalent of a guy saying he would phone you when he hadn't the slightest intention of doing so, only *she* hadn't recognised the reality. No, Darcy reflected with a stark shudder of remembrance, she had been much happier since she had given up on all that ghastly embarrassing and confusing man-woman stuff.

And if Luca, whoever he was, decided to go ahead and accept her proposition, she would soon be able to tune him and his macho motorbike leathers out entirely…

Perspiration beading her brow, Darcy wielded the heavy power-saw with the driven energy of necessity. The ancient kitchen range had an insatiable appetite for wood. Breathing heavily, she stopped to take a break. Even after switching off the saw, her ears still rang with the shattering roar of the petrol-driven motor. With a weary sigh, she bent and began laboriously stacking the logs into the waiting wheelbarrow.

'Darcy...?'

At the sound of that purring, accented drawl, Darcy almost leapt out of her skin, and she jerked round with a muttered exclamation. Luca stood several feet away. Her startled green eyes clung to his tall, outrageously masculine physique. Wide shoulders, sleek hips, long, long legs. *And* he had shaved.

One look at the to-die-for features now revealed in all their glory struck Darcy dumb. She wasn't even capable of controlling that reaction. In full daylight, he was so staggeringly handsome. High, chiselled cheekbones, sharp as blades, were dissected by an arrogant but classic nose and embellished by a wide, perfect mouth. Even his skin had that wonderful golden glowing vibrancy of warmer climes...

'Is there something wrong?' An equally shapely ebony brow had now quirked enquiringly.

'You startled me...' Heated colour drenching her skin as she realised that she had been staring, Darcy dragged her attention from him with considerable difficulty. As her dazed eyes dropped down, she blinked in disbelief at the sight of her cocker spaniels seated silently at his feet like the well trained dogs they unfortunately weren't. Strangers usually provoked Humpf and Bert into a positive frenzy of uncontrolled barking. Instead, her lovable but noisy animals were welded to the spot and throwing Luca upward pleading doggy glances as if he had cast some weird sort of hypnotic spell over them.

'I wasn't expecting you,' Darcy said abruptly.

'I did try the front entrance first...' His deep-pitched sexy drawl petered out as he studied the sizeable stack of wood. 'Surely you haven't cut all that on your own?'

Threading an even more self-conscious hand through the

damp and wildly curling tendrils of hair clinging to her forehead, she nodded, aware of the incredulity in those piercing dark eyes.

'Are there no men around here?'

'No, I'm the next best thing…but then that's nothing new,' Darcy muttered half under her breath, writhing at her own undeniable awkwardness around men and hating him for surprising her when she wasn't psyched up to deal with him.

Forgivably thrown by that odd response, Luca frowned.

Darcy leapt straight back into speech. 'I assumed you would phone—'

'Nobody ever answers your phone.'

'I'm outdoors a lot of the time.' Stripping off her heavy gloves, Darcy flexed small and painfully stiff fingers and averted her scrutiny from him, her unease in his presence pronounced. What on earth was the matter with her? She was behaving like a silly teenager with a crush. 'You'd better come inside.'

Hurriedly grabbing up an armful of logs, Darcy led the way. The long, cobbled passageway that provided a far from convenient rear entrance to her home was dark and gloomy and flanked by a multitude of closed doors. Innumerable rooms which had once enjoyed specific functions as part of the kitchen quarters now lay unused. But not for much longer, she reminded herself. When she achieved her dream of opening up the house to the public all those rooms full of their ancient labour intensive equipment would fascinate children.

And she *was* going to achieve her dream, she told herself feverishly. Surely Luca wouldn't take the trouble to make a second personal appearance if he intended to say no?

She trod into the vast echoing kitchen and knelt down by the big range at the far end. Opening the door, she thrust a sizeable log into the fuel bed. 'Did you come all the way from London again?'

'No, I stayed in Penzance last night.'

Darcy was so rigid with nervous tension, she couldn't bring herself to look at him as she breathed tautly, 'So what's your answer?'

'Yes. My answer is *yes*,' he murmured with quiet emphasis.

Her strained eyes prickled with sudden tears and she blinked rapidly before slamming shut the door on the range. The relief was so immense she felt quite dizzy for a few seconds. Feeling as if a huge weight had dropped from her shoulders, Darcy scrambled upright and turned, a grateful smile on her now softened face. 'That's great…that's really great. Would you like some coffee?'

Lounging back against the edge of the giant scrubbed pine table, Luca stared back at her, not a muscle moving in his strong dark face. It was a rather daunting reaction and she swallowed hard, unaware that that shy and spontaneous air of sudden friendliness had disconcerted him.

'OK…why not?' he agreed, without any expression at all.

Darcy put on the kettle and stole an uneasy glance at him in the taut silence. She didn't know where the tension was coming from, and then she wondered if his brooding silence was a kind of male ego thing. 'I suppose this isn't quite the sort of work you were hoping to get,' she conceded awkwardly. 'But I promise you that you won't regret it. How long have you been unemployed?'

'Unemployed?' he echoed, strong features stiffening.

'Sorry, I just assumed—'

'I have never been employed in the UK.'

'*Oh…*' Darcy nodded slowly. 'So how long have you been over here?'

'Long enough…'

Darcy scrutinised that slightly downbent dark glossy head, taking in the faint darkening of colour over his sculpted cheekbones. He was embarrassed at his lack of success in the job market, she gathered, and she wished she had been a little less blunt in her questioning. But then tact had never been her strong point. And when she had interviewed him she had been so wrapped up in her own problems that it hadn't occurred to her that Luca must have been desperate to find a job to come so far out of London in answer to one small ad. Furthermore, now that she took a closer look at those leathers of his, she couldn't help but notice that they were pretty worn.

Sudden sympathy swept Darcy. She knew all about being broke and trying to keep up appearances. She had looked down on him for wearing motorbike gear to an interview, but maybe the poor guy didn't have much else to wear. If he hadn't worked since he had arrived in the UK, he certainly couldn't have financed much of a wardrobe. Smart suits cost money.

'I'll give you half your first month's salary in advance,' Darcy heard herself say. 'As a sort of retainer...'

This time he looked frankly startled.

'You probably think that's very trusting of me, but I tend to take people as I find them. In any case, I don't have a lot of choice *but* to trust you. If you were to get the chance of another job and decide to back out on me, I'd be in trouble,' she said honestly. 'How do you like your coffee?'

'Black...two sugars.'

Darcy put a pile of biscuits on a rather chipped plate. Setting the two beakers of coffee down on the table, she sat down and reached for the jotter and pencil lying there. 'I'd better get some details from you, hadn't I? What *is* your surname?'

There was a pause, a distinct pause as he sank lithely down opposite her.

'Raffacani...' he breathed.

'You'll need to spell that for me.'

He obliged.

Darcy bent industriously over the jotter. 'And Luca—is that your first and only other name? You see, I have to get this right for the vicar.'

'Gianluca...Gianluca Fabrizio.'

'I think you'd better spell all of it.' She took down his birthdate. Raffacani, she was thinking. Why did she have the curious sense that she had come across that name somewhere before? She shook her head. For all she knew Raffacani was as common a name in Italy as Smith was in England.

'Right,' she said then. 'I'll contact my solicitor, Mr Stevens. He's based in Penzance, so you can sign the prenuptial contract as soon as you like. Those references you offered...?'

From the inside of his jacket he withdrew a somewhat creased envelope. Struggling to keep up a businesslike attitude when she really just wanted to sing and dance round the kitchen with relief, Darcy withdrew the documents. There were two, one with a very impressive letterhead, but both were written in Italian. 'I'll hang onto these and study them,' she told him, thinking of the old set of foreign language dictionaries in the library. 'But I'm sure they'll be fine.'

'How soon do you envisage the marriage ceremony taking place?' Luca Raffacani enquired.

'Hopefully in about three weeks. It'll be a very quiet wedding,' Darcy explained rather stiffly, fixing her attention to the scarred surface of the table, her face turning pale and set. 'But as my father died this year that won't surprise anyone. It wouldn't be quite the thing to have a big splash.'

'You're not inviting many guests?'

'Actually...' Darcy breathed in deep, plunged into dismal recall of the huge misfired wedding which her father had insisted on staging three years earlier. 'Well, actually, I wasn't planning on inviting anybody,' she admitted tightly as she rose restively to her feet again. 'I'll show you where you'll be staying when you move in, shall I?'

At an infinitely more graceful and leisurely pace, Luca slid upright and straightened. Darcy watched in helpless fascination. His every movement had such...such *style,* an unhurried cool that caught the eye. He was so self-possessed, so contained. He was also very reserved. He gave nothing away. Well, would she have preferred a garrulous extrovert who asked a lot of awkward questions? Irritated by her own growing curiosity, Darcy left him to follow her out of the kitchen and tried to concentrate on more important things.

'What did you mean when you said you were the next best thing to a man around here?' Luca enquired on the way up the grand oak staircase.

'My father wanted a son, not a daughter—at least...not the kind of daughter I turned out to be.' As she spoke, Darcy was comparing herself to her stepsister. Morton Fielding had been utterly charmed by his second wife's beautiful daughter, Nina. Darcy had looked on in amazement as Nina twisted her cold and censorious parent round her little finger with ease.

'Your mother?'

'She died when I was six. I hardly remember her,' Darcy confided ruefully. 'My father remarried a few years later. He was desperate to have a male heir but I'm afraid it didn't happen.'

She cast open the door of a big dark oak-panelled bedroom, dominated by a giant Elizabethan four-poster. 'This will be your room. The bathroom's through that door. I'm afraid we'll have to share it. There isn't another one on this side of the house.'

As he glanced round the sparsely furnished and decidedly dusty room, which might have figured in a Tudor time warp, Darcy found herself studying him again. That stunningly male profile, the hard, sleek lines of his muscular length. A tiny frisson of sexual heat tightened her stomach muscles. He strolled with the grace of a leopard over to the high casement window to look out. Sunlight gleamed over his luxuriant black hair. Unexpectedly he turned, dark eyes with the dramatic impact of gold resting on her in cool enquiry.

Caught watching him again, Darcy blushed as hotly as

an embarrassed schoolgirl. She was appalled by her own outrageous physical awareness of him, could not comprehend what madness was dredging such responses from her. Whirling round, she walked swiftly back into the corridor.

As he drew level with her she snatched in a deep, sustaining breath and started towards the stairs again. 'I'm afraid there are very few modern comforts in the Folly, and locally, well, there's even fewer social outlets...' She hesitated uneasily before continuing, 'What I'm really trying to say is that if you feel the need to take off for the odd day in search of amusement, I'll understand—'

'Amusement?' Luca prompted grimly, as if such a concept had never come his way before.

Darcy nodded, staring stonily ahead. 'I'm one of these people who always says exactly what's on their mind. I live very quietly but I can't reasonably expect you to do the same thing for an entire six months. I'm sure you'll maybe want to go up to London occasionally and—'

'Amuse myself?' Luca slotted in very drily.

In spite of her discomfiture, Darcy uttered a strained little laugh. 'You can hardly bring a girlfriend here—'

'I do not have a woman in my life,' he interrupted, with a strong suggestion of gritted teeth.

'Possibly not at present,' Darcy allowed, wondering what on earth was the matter with him. He was reacting as if she had grossly insulted him in some way. 'But I'm being realistic. You're bound to get bored down here. City slickers do...'

Brilliant eyes black as jet stabbed into her. A line of dark colour now lay over his taut cheekbones. 'There will not be a woman nor any need for such behaviour on my part, I assure you,' he imparted icily.

They were descending the stairs when a tiny figure clad in bright red leggings and a yellow T-shirt appeared in the Great Hall below. 'Mummy!' Zia carrolled with exuberance.

As her daughter flashed over to eagerly show off a much

creased painting, Luca fell still. Interpreting his silence as astonishment, Darcy flung him an apologetic glance as she lifted her daughter up into her arms. 'My daughter, Zia…I hadn't got around to mentioning her yet,' she conceded rather defensively.

Luca slid up a broad shoulder in an infinitesimal shrug of innate elegance. The advent of a stray cat might have inspired as much interest. Not a male who had any time for children, Darcy gathered, resolving to ensure that her playful and chatty toddler was kept well out of his path.

'Is there anything else you wish to discuss?' Luca prompted with faint impatience.

Darcy stiffened. Minutes later, she had written and passed him the cheque she had promised. He folded the item and tucked it into his inside pocket with complete cool. 'I'll drop you a note as soon as I get the date of the ceremony organised. I won't need to see you again before that,' she told him.

Luca printed a phone number on the front of the jotter she had left lying. 'If you need to contact me for any other reason, leave a message on that line.'

A fortnight later, Darcy unbolted the huge front door of the Folly and dragged it open, only to freeze in dismay.

'About time too,' Margo Fielding complained sharply as she swept past, reeking of expensive perfume and irritation, closely followed by her daughter, Nina.

Aghast at the unforewarned descent of her stepmother and her stepsister, Darcy watched with a sinking heart as the tall, beautiful blonde duo stalked ahead of her into the drawing room.

She hadn't laid eyes on either woman since they had moved out after her father's funeral, eager to leave the privations of country life behind them and return to city life. The discovery that Darcy could not be forced to sell the Folly and share the proceeds with them had led to a strained parting of the ways. Although Morton Fielding had generously provided for his widow, and Margo was a wealthy woman in her own right, her stepmother had been far from satisfied.

Margo cast her an outraged look. 'Don't you think you should've told me that you were getting married?' she demanded as she took up a painfully familiar bullying stance at the fireplace. 'Can you imagine how I felt when a friend called me to ask *who* you were marrying and I had to confess my ignorance? How dare you embarrass me like that?'

Darcy was very tense, her tummy muscles knotting up while she wondered how on earth the older woman had discovered her plans. The vicar's wife could be a bit of a gossip, she conceded, and Margo still had friends locally. No doubt that was how word had travelled farther afield at such speed. 'I'm sorry…I would've informed you after the wedding—'

Nina's scornful blue eyes raked over the younger woman. 'But of course, *when* it's safely over. You're terrified that your bridegroom will bolt last minute, like Richard did!'

At that unpleasant and needless reminder, which was painfully apt, the embarrassed colour drained from Darcy's taut cheekbones. 'I—'

'Just when I thought you must finally be coming to your senses and accepting the need to sell this white elephant of a house, you suddenly decide to get married,' Margo condemned with stark resentment. 'Is *he* even presentable?'

'With all this heavy secrecy, it's my bet that the groom is totally *un*presentable…one of the estate workers?' Nina suggested, with a disdainful little shudder of snobbish distaste.

'You're not pregnant again, are you?' Margo treated Darcy to a withering and accusing appraisal. 'That's what people are going to think. And I *refuse* to have my acquaintance view me as some sort of wicked stepmother! So you'll have to pay for a proper wedding reception and I'll act as your hostess.'

'I'm afraid I haven't got the money for that,' Darcy admitted tightly.

'What about *him?*' Nina pressed instantaneously.

Darcy flushed and looked away.

'Penniless, I suppose.' Reaching that conclusion, Margo exchanged a covert look of relief and satisfaction with her daughter. 'I do hope he's aware that when you go bust here, we're entitled to a slice of whatever is left.'

'I'm not planning to go bust,' Darcy breathed, her taut fingers clenching in on themselves.

'I'm just dying to meet this character.' Nina giggled. 'Who is he?'

'His name's Luca—'

'What kind of a name is that?' her stepmother demanded.

'He's Italian,' Darcy confided grudgingly.

'An immigrant?' Nina squealed, as if that was the funniest thing she had ever heard. 'I do hope he's not marrying you just to get a British passport!'

'I'll throw a small engagement party for you this weekend in Truro,' Margo announced grandly with a glacial smile. 'I will not have people say that I didn't at least *try* to do my duty by my late husband's child.'

'That's very kind of you,' Darcy mumbled, after a staggered pause at the fact that Margo was prepared to make so much effort on her behalf. 'But—'

'No buts, Darcy. Everyone knows how eccentric you are, but I will not allow you to embarrass me in front of my friends. I will expect you and your fiancé at eight on Friday, *both* of you suitably dressed. And if he's as hopeless as you are in polite company, tell him to keep his mouth shut and just smile.'

Her expectations voiced, Margo was already sweeping out to the hall. Darcy unfroze and sped after her. 'But Luca...Luca's got other arrangements for that night!' she lied in a frantic rush.

'Saturday, then,' Margo decreed instead.

Darcy's tremulous lips sealed again. How could she refuse to produce her supposed fiancé without giving the impression that there was something most peculiar about their relationship? She should never have practised such secrecy, never have surrendered to her own shrinking reluctance to make any form of public appearance with a man in tow. In her position, she couldn't afford to arouse suspicion that there was anything strange about her forthcoming marriage.

'I'm so glad you've finally found yourself a man.' Nina dealt her a pitying look of superiority. 'What does he do for a living?'

Darcy hesitated. She just couldn't bring herself to admit that Luca was unemployed. 'He...he works in a bank.'

'A clerk...how *sweet*. Love blossomed over the counter, did it?'

Utterly drained, and annoyed that she had allowed her stepmother to reduce her yet again to a state of dumbstruck inadequacy, Darcy stood as the two women climbed into their sleek, expensive BMW and drove off without further ado.

'Luca, haven't you got *any* of my other messages? I realise that this is terribly short notice, but I do really *need* you to show up with me at this party in Truro...er...our engagement party,' Darcy stated apologetically to the answering machine which greeted her for the frustrating fourth time at the London number he had left with her. 'This is an emergency. Saturday night at eight. Could you get in touch, please?'

'The toad's done a bunk on you with that cheque!' Karen groaned in despair. 'I don't know why you agreed to this party anyway. Margo and Nina have to be up to something. They've never done you a favour in their lives. And if Luca fails to show up, those two witches will have a terrific laugh at your expense!'

'There's still twenty-four hours to go. I'm sure I'll hear from him soon,' Darcy muttered fiercely, refusing to give up hope as she hugged Zia, grateful for the comforting warmth of her sturdy little body next to her own.

'Darcy…you have written to him as well. He is obviously not at home and if he is home, he's ignoring you—'

'I don't think he's like that, Karen,' Darcy objected, suddenly feeling more than a little irritated with her friend for running Luca down and forecasting the worst. From what she had contrived to roughly translate of her future husband's references, one of which was persuasively written by a high court judge, she was dealing with a male of considerable integrity and sterling character.

Late that night the frustratingly silent phone finally rang and Darcy raced like a maniac to answer it. *'Yes?'* she gasped with breathless hope into the receiver.

'Luca… I got your messages this evening—all of them.'

'Oh, thank heaven…thank heaven!' Just hearing the intensely welcome sound of that deep, dark accented drawl, Darcy went weak at the knees. 'I was starting to think I was going to have to ring my stepmother and say you'd come down with some sudden illness! She would've been absolutely furious. We've never been close, and I certainly didn't want this wretched party, but it is pretty decent of her to offer, isn't it?'

'I'm afraid we have one slight problem to overcome,' Luca slotted softly into that flood of relieved explanation. 'I'm calling from Italy.'

'Italy…?' Darcy blinked rapidly, thoroughly thrown by the announcement. *'It-Italy?'* she stammered in horror.

'But naturally I will do my utmost to get back in time for the party,' Luca assured her in a tone of cool assurance.

Darcy sighed heavily then, unsurprised by his coolness. What right did she have to muck up his arrangements? This whole mess wasn't his fault, it was hers. After all, she had told him she wouldn't need to see him again before the wedding. Obviously he had used the money she had given him to travel home and see his family. 'I'm really sorry about this,' she said tiredly, the stress of several sleepless nights edging her voice. 'Look, *can* you make it?'

'With the best will in the world, not to the party before nine in the evening...unless you want to meet me there?' he suggested.

Aghast at the idea of arriving alone, Darcy uttered an instant negative.

'Then offer my apologies to your stepmother. I'll come and pick you up.'

Darcy told herself that she was incredibly lucky that Luca was willing to come back from Italy to attend the party at such short notice. 'I really appreciate this...look, you can stay here on Saturday night,' she offered gratefully. 'I'll make up the bed for you.'

'That's extraordinarily kind of you, Darcy,' Luca drawled smoothly.

# CHAPTER THREE

ZIA was spending the night with Karen in the gatehouse. Returning to the Folly to nervously await Luca's arrival, Darcy caught an unsought glimpse of her reflection in the giant mirror in the echoing hall…

And suddenly she was wishing she had spent money she could ill afford on a new outfit. The brown dress hung loose round her hips and flapped to an indeterminate length below her knees. The ruffled neckline, once chosen to conceal the embarrassing smallness of her breasts, looked fussy and old-fashioned. She was much more comfortable in trousers—never had had much luck in choosing clothes that flattered her slight and diminutive frame…

And in the back of her wardrobe the green designer evening dress which had been Maxie's wedding present three years earlier still hung, complete with shoes and delicate little beaded bag. Maxie, no longer a friend and always rather too reserved and too confident of her feminine attraction for Darcy to feel quite comfortable in her radius. As for the dress, Darcy hadn't looked near it once since her return from Venice. She needed no reminder of that night of explosive passion in a stranger's arms. Yet somehow she still hadn't been able to bring herself to dispose of that exquisite gown which had lent her the miraculous illusion of beauty for a few brief hours.

The Victorian bell-pull shrieked complaint in the piercing silence, springing Darcy out of a past that still felt all too recent and all too wounding. In haste, she yanked open the heavy door. There she stopped dead at the sight of Luca, her witch-green eyes widening to their fullest extent in unconcealed surprise.

He was wearing a supremely elegant black dinner jacket when she hadn't dared even to ask if he possessed such an article. And there he stood, proud black head high, strong dark face assured, one lean brown hand negligently thrust into the pocket of narrow black trousers to tighten them over his lean hips and long powerful thighs, his beautifully tailored jacket parted to reveal a pristine white pleated dress shirt. He looked so incredibly sophisticated and gorgeous he stole the breath from Darcy's convulsing throat.

'Gosh, you hired evening dress,' she mumbled, relocating her vocal cords with difficulty.

Luca ran brilliant dark eyes over her, a distinct frownline drawing together his ebony brows. 'Possibly I'm slightly over-dressed for the occasion?'

'No…no…not at all.' Never more self-conscious than when her personal appearance was under scrutiny, Darcy flushed to the roots of her hair. Her attention abruptly fell on the glossy scarlet Porsche sitting parked beside the ancient Land Rover which was her only means of transport. 'Where on earth did you get that car?' she gasped helplessly.

'It's on loan.'

Slowly, Darcy shook her curly auburn head. It would be madness to turn up in an expensive car and give a false impression of Luca's standing in the world. Margo would ask five hundred questions and soon penetrate the truth. Then Luca, who could only have borrowed the car for her benefit—and she couldn't help but be touched by that realisation—would end up feeling cut off. 'I would really love to roar up in the Porsche, but it would be wiser to use the Land Rover,' she told him in some disappointment.

'*Dio mio…* you are joking, of course.' Luca surveyed the rusting and battered four-wheel drive with outright incredulity. 'It's a wreck.'

Darcy opened the door of the Land Rover. 'I do know what I'm talking about, Luca,' she warned. 'If we show up in the Porsche, my stepmother will get entirely the wrong idea and decide that you're loaded. If we're anything less than honest, we'll both be left sitting with egg on our faces. We want to blend in, not create comment, and that car must be worth about thirty thousand—'

'Seventy.'

'*Seventy* thousand pounds?' Darcy broke in, her disbelief writ large in her shaken face.

'And some change,' Luca completed drily.

'Wish I had a friend willing to trust me with a car like that! We'll park the Land Rover out on the road and run away from it fast,' Darcy promised, worriedly examining her watch and then climbing into the driver's seat to forestall further argument. 'I'd let you drive, but this old girl has a number of idiocyncrasies which might irritate you.'

'This is ridiculous,' Luca swung into the tatty passenger seat with pronounced reluctance, his classic profile hard as a granite cliff in winter.

As she stole a second glance at that hawkish masculine profile, Darcy found herself thinking that he had a kind of Heathcliffish rough edge when he was angry.

And he *was* definitely angry, and she didn't mind in the slightest. It made him seem far more human. Posh cars and men and their egos, she reflected with sudden good cheer. Even *she* understood that basic connection. 'Believe me, you're about to cause enough of a stir tonight. You're very good-looking…'

'Am I really?' Luca prompted rather flatly.

'Oh, come on, no false modesty. I bet you've been breaking hearts from the edge of the cradle!' Darcy riposted with a rueful sound of amusement.

'You're very frank.'

'In that garb you look like you just strolled in off a movie set,' Darcy reeled off, trying to work herself up to giving the little speech she had planned. 'Do you think you could contrive to act like you're keen on me tonight? No…no, don't say anything,' she urged with a distinctly embarrassed laugh. 'It's just that nobody can smell a rat faster than

Margo or Nina, and you are not at all what they are primed to expect.'

'What are they expecting?'

'Some ordinary boring guy who works in a bank.'

'Where do you get the idea that bankers are boring?'

'My bank manager could bore for Britain. Every time I walk into his office, he acts like I'm there to steal from him. That man is just such a pessimist,' Darcy rattled on, grateful to have got over the hint about him acting keen without further discussion. It was so unbelievably embarrassing to have to ask a man to put on such a pretence. 'When he tells me the size of my overdraft, he even reads out the pence owing to make me squirm—'

'You have an overdraft?'

'It's not as bad as it sounds. The day we get married, I will have some really good news for my bank manager…at least I hope he thinks it's good news, and loosens the purse-strings a little.' She shot him an apprehensive glance, wishing she hadn't allowed nervous tension to tempt her into such dangerous candour. 'Don't worry, if the worst comes to the worst, I could always sell something to keep the bank quiet. I made a commitment to you and I won't let you down.'

'I'm impressed. Tell me, have you thought of a cover story for this evening?' Luca enquired with some satire.

'Cover story?'

'Where and how we met, et cetera, et cetera.'

'Of course,' she said in some surprise. 'We'll say we met in London. I haven't been there in over a year, but they're not likely to know that. I want to give the impression that we've plunged into one of those sudden whirlwind romances and then, when we split up, nobody will be the slightest bit surprised.'

'I see you're wearing a ring.'

'It's on loan, like your Porsche. We can't act engaged without a ring.' Darcy had borrowed the diamond dress ring from Karen for the evening, and her finger had been

crooked ever since it went on because it was a size too big
and she was totally terrified of losing it.

'Don't you think you ought to fill me in on a few background details on your family? My younger sister is the
only close relative I have,' he revealed. 'She's a student.'

'Oh…right. My stepmother, Margo, was first married to
a wealthy businessman with one foot in the grave. They
had a daughter, Nina, who's a model,' she shared. 'Margo
married my father for social position; he married her in the
hope of having a son. Dad was always very tight with
money, but Margo and Nina could squeeze juice out of a
dehydrated lemon. He was extremely generous to them.
That's one of the reasons the estate is in such a mess…I
inherited the mess and a load of death duties.'

'Very succinct,' Luca responded with a slight catch in
his voice.

'Margo and Nina are frantic snobs. They spend the summer in Truro and the rest of the year in their London apartment. Margo doesn't like me but she loves throwing parties,
and she is very, very conscious of what other people think.'

'Are you?'

'Good heavens, no, as an unmarried mother, I can hardly
afford to be!'

'I think I should at least know the name of the father of
your child,' Luca remarked.

The silence in the car became electric. Darcy accelerated
down the road, small hands clenching the steering wheel
tightly. 'On that point, I'm afraid I've never gratified anyone's curiosity,' she said stiffly, and after that uncompro-
mising snub the silence lasted all the way to Truro.

Some distance from her stepmother's large detached
home, which was set within its own landscaped grounds on
the outskirts of town, Darcy nudged her vehicle into a
space. And only with difficulty. They walked up the sweeping drive and Darcy's heart sank as she took in the number
of cars already parked. 'I think there's going to be a lot
more people here than I was led to expect. If anyone asks

too many probing questions, pretend your English is lousy,'
she advised nervously.

'I believe I will cope.' Luca curved a confident hand over
her tense spine. Her flesh tingled below the thin fabric of
her dress and she shivered. He bent his glossy dark head
down almost to her level, quite a feat with the difference
in their heights. The faint scent of some citrus-based lotion
flared Darcy's sensitive nostrils. Her breath tripping in her
throat, she collided with deep, dark flashing eyes and her
stomach turned a shaken somersault in reaction.

*'Per meraviglia…'* Luca breathed with deflating cool
and impatience. 'Will you at least smile as if you're happy?
And stop hunching your shoulders like that. Walk tall!'

Plunged back to harsh reality with a jolt, her colour considerably heightened, Darcy might have made a pithy retort
had not Margo's housekeeper swept open the door for their
entrance.

And entrance it certainly was. Margo and Nina were in
the hall, chatting in a group. Their eyes flew to Darcy, and
then straight past her to the tall, spectacularly noticeable
male by her side. Her stepmother and her stepsister stilled
in astonishment and simply stared. Suddenly Darcy was
wickedly amused. Luca was undeniably presentable. How
unexpectedly sweet it was to surprise the two women
whose constant criticisms and cutting comments had made
her teenage years such a misery.

Retaining that light hold on her, Luca carried her forward.

'Darcy…Luca,' Margo said rather stiltedly.

After waiting in vain for Darcy to make an introduction,
Luca advanced a hand and murmured calmly, 'Luca
Raffacani, Mrs Fielding…I'm delighted to meet you at
last.'

'Margo, *please,*' her stepmother gushed.

Nina hovered in a revealing little slip dress, her beautiful
face etched with a rigid smile while her pale blue eyes ran
over Luca as if he was a large piece of her own lost prop-

erty. 'I'm surprised...you don't look remotely like Richard,' she remarked. 'I was so sure you'd be horsy and hearty. Darcy always did go for the outdoor type.'

'Richard?' Luca queried.

'Oh, dear, I do hope I haven't been indiscreet,' Nina murmured with a little moue of fake dismay. 'Sorry, but I naturally assumed you would know that Darcy was engaged once before—'

'Left at the altar too. A ghastly business altogether. That's why it's so wonderful to see you happy now, Darcy!' Margo continued.

Darcy cringed as if her dress had fallen off in public, unable to look anywhere near Luca to see how he was reacting to this humiliating information. Her stepmother took advantage of her disconcertion to rest a welcoming hand on Luca's sleeve and neatly impose herself between them.

'Oh, do let us see the ring,' Nina trilled.

Darcy extended her hand. An insincere chorus of compliments followed.

They moved into a large reception room which was filled to the gills with chattering, elegantly dressed people. Margo turned to address Luca in a confidential aside. 'I'm really hoping that marriage will give Darcy something more to think about than that pile of bricks and mortar she's so obsessively attached to. What *do* you think of Fielding's Folly, Luca?'

'It's Darcy's home and of obvious historic interest—'

'But such a dreadful ceaseless drain on one's financial resources, and a simply *huge* responsibility. You'll soon find that out,' Margo warned him feelingly. 'Worry drove my poor husband to an early death. It's always the same with these old families. Land-rich, cash-poor. Morton was almost as stubborn as Darcy, but I don't think he ever dreamt that she would go to such nonsensical lengths to try and hang on to the estate—'

'I don't think we need to discuss this right now,' Darcy broke in tautly.

'It has to be said, darling, and your fiancé *is* part of the family now,' her stepmother pointed out loftily. 'After all, I'm only thinking of your future, and Luca does have a right to know what he's getting into. No doubt you've given him a *very* rosy picture, and really that's not very fair—'

'Not at all. I have an excellent understanding of how matters stand on the estate,' Luca inserted with smiling calm as he eased away from the older woman and extended a hand to Darcy, closing long fingers over hers to tug her close again, as if he couldn't quite bear to be physically separated from her.

'That's right. You work in the financial field,' Nina commented with a look of amusement. 'I can hardly believe you're only a bank clerk...'

'Neither can I. Darcy...what *have* you been telling this family of yours?' Luca scolded with a husky laugh of amusement. 'Pressure of work persuaded me to take what you might call a sabbatical here in the UK. Meeting Darcy, a woman so very much after my own heart, was a quite unexpected bonus.'

'How on earth *did* you meet?'

'I'm not sure I should tell you...' Luca responded in a teasing undertone.

'Feel free,' Darcy encouraged, already staggered by the ease with which he was entertaining and dealing with Margo and Nina. Yet he had been so very, very quiet with her. But then why was she surprised at that? Her soft mouth tightened. Here he was with two lovely, admiring women hanging on his very word; quite naturally he was opening up and no longer either bored and impatient.

'OK. It happened in London. She reversed into my car and then got out and shouted at me. I really appreciate a woman with that much nerve!' Luca divulged playfully, and Darcy's bright head flew up in shock. 'You do everything behind the wheel at such frantic speed, don't you, *cara mia?* I wanted to strangle her, and then I wanted to kiss her...'

'Which did you do?' Darcy heard herself prompt, unnerved by his sheer inventiveness.

'I believe *some* things should remain private...' To accompany that low-pitched and sensually suggestive murmur, Luca ran a long brown forefinger along her delicate jawbone in a glancing caress. Darcy gazed up at him, all hot pink and overpowered, every muscle in her slender length tensing. Her tender flesh stung in the wake of that easy touch, leaving her maddeningly, insanely aware of his powerful masculinity.

'To think I used to believe my little stepsister was painfully shy,' Nina breathed, fascinated against her will by this show of intimacy.

'Hardly, when she's already the mother of a noisy toddler,' Margo put in cuttingly. 'Do you like children, Luca?'

'I *adore* them,' he drawled, with positive fervour.

'How wonderful,' Margo said rather weakly, having shot her last bitchy bolt and found him impregnable. 'Let me introduce you to our guests, Luca. Don't be so possessive, Darcy. Do let go of the poor man for a second.'

Darcy yanked her hand from Luca's sleeve. She hadn't even realised she had been hanging onto him. Feeling slightly disorientated, she watched as he deftly reached for the glasses of champagne offered by one of the catering staff.

She studied those lean brown hands, the beautifully shaped long fingers and polished nails. She recalled the smoothness of that fingertip dancing along her oversensitive jawbone, sending tiny little tremors down her rigid spine with an innate sensuality that mesmerised. And for the shocking space of one crashing heartbeat, as she met those astonishing dark golden eyes in concert, there had been nobody and nothing else in the room for her.

'You're not making much effort, are you?' Luca gritted in her ear.

'I never challenge Margo if I can help it,' she whispered back. 'She fights back with my most embarrassing moments. I learnt that lesson years ago.'

'Strange...you didn't strike me as a woman who lies down to get kicked.'

Darcy flinched at that damning retaliation. 'Excuse me,' she muttered, and hurried off into the cool of the less crowded hall.

'You won't hold onto that guy for ten seconds,' a sharp voice forecast nastily from the rear. 'I can't think what he imagines he sees in you, but he'll soon find out he's made a big mistake.'

Darcy swung round to face her stepsister. 'Time will no doubt tell.'

'Luca's not even your type,' Nina snapped resentfully. 'How long do you think you're likely to hold off the opposition? He doesn't look dirt-poor to me either. I know clothes, and what he's wearing did not come out of any charity shop.'

'Luca likes to dress well.' Darcy shrugged.

'A peacock with a dull little peahen fluttering in his wake?' Nina sneered. 'He'll soon be out looking for more excitement. No, if there's one thing I'm convinced of now that I've seen him, it's that he's playing a double game. It *has* to be the British passport he's after...why else would he be marrying you?'

Why else? Darcy repeated inwardly as Nina stalked off again. What a huge laugh Margo and Nina would have were they ever to discover that Luca was no more than a somewhat unusual paid employee, prepared to act out a masquerade for six months. And every word her stepsister had spoken was painfully true. In the normal way of things a male of Luca's ilk would *not* have looked at her twice.

'Darcy...' Luca was poised several feet away, a slanting smile for show on his beautiful mouth and exasperation glittering in his deep-set dark eyes. 'I wondered where you had got to.'

He could act. Dear heaven, but he could act, Darcy found herself acknowledging over the next few hours. He kept her beside him, dragged her into the conversation and paid her every possible attention. Yet increasingly Darcy became more occupied in watching and listening to *him*.

In vain did she strive to recapture the image of the far from chatty male in motorbike leathers. For Luca Raffacani appeared to be a chameleon. With the donning of that dinner jacket, he appeared to have slid effortlessly into a new persona.

Now she saw a male possessed of a startling degree of sophistication and supremely at his ease in social company. He was adroit at sidestepping too personal enquiries. He was cool as ice, extremely witty and, she began to think, almost frighteningly clever. And other people were equally impressed. He gathered a crowd. Far from blending in, Luca commanded attention.

At one in the morning, he walked her into the conservatory, where several couples were dancing, and complained, 'You've been incredibly quiet.'

'And you're surprised?' Darcy stared up at him and stepped back. In the dim light, his lean, dark face had a saturnine quality. Brilliant eyes raked over her as keen and sharp as laser beams. 'You're like Jekyll and Hyde. I feel like I don't know you at all—'

'You don't,' Luca agreed.

'And yet you don't quite fit in here either,' she murmured uncertainly, speaking her thoughts out loud and yet unable to properly put them together. 'You stand out too much somehow.'

'That's your imagination talking,' Luca asserted with a smoky laugh as he encircled her with his arms.

He curved his palm to the base of her spine and drew her close. Her breasts rubbed against his shirt-front. A current of heat darted through her and she felt her nipples spring into murderously tight and prominent buds. She went rigid with discomfiture. 'Relax,' he urged from above her head. 'Margo is watching. We're supposed to be lovers, not strangers…'

The indefinable scent of him engulfed her. Clean and warm and very male. She quivered, struggling to loosen her taut muscles and shamefully aware of every slight movement of his big, powerful body. She wanted to sink in to the hard masculinity of him, but she held herself back, and in so doing missed a step. To compensate, he had to bring her even closer.

'I'm not a great dancer,' she muttered in a mortified apology.

'*Dio mio*…you move like air in my arms,' he countered.

And in his arms, amazingly, she did, absorbed as one into the animal grace and natural rhythm with which he whirled her round the floor. It was like flying, she thought dreamily, and the reflection could only rekindle a fairy tale memory of dancing on a balcony high above the Grand Canal in Venice. No wrong steps, no awkwardness, no need even for conversation—just the sheer joy of moving in perfect synchronisation with the music.

'You dance like a dream,' she whispered breathlessly in the split second after the music stopped, and she found herself as someone unwilling to awake from that dream, plastered as surely as melted cheese on toast to every abrasive angle of his lean, hard body.

Somehow her arms had crept up round his neck, and her fingers were flirting deliciously with his thick silky black hair. Unnaturally still now, she gazed up at him, green eyes huge pools of growing confusion. Dear heaven, those eyes of his. Even semi-screened with luxuriant black lashes, their impact was animal direct and splinteringly sensual.

As his arrogant dark head lowered, her breath feathered in her throat. But she was still stunned when he actually kissed her. He parted her lips with his and took her soft mouth with a driving, hungry assurance that blistered through every shocked atom of her being with the efficiency of a lightning bolt. In the very act of detaching her fingers from his hair she clung instead, clung to stay upright, vaguely attached to planet earth even though she was no longer aware of its existence.

Heat engulfed her sensation-starved body, swelling her breasts, pinching her nipples into distended prominence and sending a flash-flood of fire cascading down between her quivering thighs. As his tongue searched out the yielding tender sensitivity of her mouth, raw excitement scorched to such heights inside her she was convinced she was burning alive.

Luca lifted his hips from hers, surveyed her blitzed expression and dealt her a curiously hard but amused look. 'Time to leave,' he informed her lazily. 'I believe we've played our part well enough to satisfy.'

As Luca spun her under the shelter of one seemingly possessive arm and walked her off the floor, Darcy was in shock. Her legs no longer felt as if they belonged to the rest of her, and she was still struggling to breath at a normal rate. In the aftermath of that passionate kiss she was a prey to conflicting and powerful reactions, the craziest of which was the momentary insane conviction that Luca and Zia's father could only be one and the same man!

Oh, dear heaven, how could she have forgotten herself to that extent? And the answer came back. He kissed like Zia's father. Earthquake-force seduction. Smooth as glass. Going for the kill like a hitman, faster on his feet than a jump-jet. She was devastated by the completeness of her own surrender, and utterly dumbfounded by that weird sense of the familiar which afflicted her, that crazy paranoiac sense of *déjà vu*...

For her Venetian lover had known nothing about her and could never have discovered her identity. Her secrecy that night had been more than a game she'd played to tantalise. She had been honestly afraid that reality would destroy the magic. After all, he had been attracted by a woman who didn't really exist. And his uninterest in further contact had been more than adequately proven when he'd left her standing on the Ponte della Guerra the following day!

Yet only he and Luca had ever had such an effect on her, awakening a shameless brand of instant overpowering lust that sent every nerve-ending and hormone into overdrive and paid not the slightest heed to self-control or moral restraint. She breathed in deep to steady herself.

Maybe all Italian men learned to kiss like that in their teens, she told herself grimly. Maybe she was just a complete push-over for Italian men—at least those of the tall, dark, well-built and sensationally desirable variety. Maybe living like a nun and refusing to recognise that she might *have* physical needs had made her a degradingly easy mark for any male with the right sensual technique.

But what was technique without chemistry? she asked herself doggedly. It was pathetic for her to try and deny one minute longer that she was wildly, dangerously attracted to Luca Raffacani. For what pride had refused to face head-on, her own body had just proved with mortifying eagerness.

As Luca thanked her stepmother for the party, Margo gave Darcy's hot cheeks a frozen look while Nina surveyed her stepsister as if she had just witnessed a poor, defenceless man being brutally attacked by a sexually starved woman. Darcy's farewells were incoherent and brief.

The night air hit her like a rejuvenating bucket of cold water. 'We've played our part well enough to satisfy,' Luca had said, only minutes earlier. At that recollection Darcy now paled and stiffened, as if she had been slapped in the face.

Naturally that kiss had simply been part of the masquerade. He had been *acting*. Acting as if he was attracted to her, in love with her, on the very brink of marrying her. Oh, dear heaven, had he guessed? Did he for one moment suspect that *she* hadn't been acting? How much could a man tell from one kiss? As kisses went, her response had been downright encouraging. Her self-respect cowered at that acknowledgement.

'That went off OK,' Luca drawled with distinct satisfaction.

'Yes, you were marvellous,' Darcy agreed, struggling to sound breezy, approving and grateful, and instead sounding as if each individual word had been wrenched from her at gun-point. 'The kiss was a real bull's-eye clincher too. Strikes me you could make a fortune as a gigolo!'

With a forced laugh, she trod ahead of him, valiantly fighting to control her growing sense of writhing mortification.

'Say that again…'

Stalking rigid-backed down the pavement, Darcy slung another not very convincing laugh over her shoulder. 'Well, you've got everything going for you in that line,' she told him with determined humour. 'The look, the charm, the patter, the screen-kiss technique. If I was some fading lonely lady with nothing but my money to keep me warm, I would've been swept off my feet in there!'

Without warning, a shockingly powerful hand linked forcibly with hers and pulled her round to face him again. Startled, Darcy looked up and clashed with blazing golden eyes as enervating as a ten-ton truck bearing down on her shrinking length.

'*Porca miseria!*' Luca growled in outrage. 'You compare me to a gigolo?'

Genuinely taken aback by that reaction, Darcy gawped at him. And then the penny dropped. Considering the monetary aspect of their private arrangement, her lack of tact now left her stricken. 'Oh, no, I never thought… I mean, I really *didn't* mean—'

'That I am a man who would sell himself for money?' Luca incised in a raw tone that told her he took himself very seriously.

Darcy was so appalled by her own thoughtlessness that her hand fluttered up between them to pluck apologetically

at his lapel and then smooth it down again. 'Luca...
*honestly,* I was just trying to be funny—'

'Ha...ha,' Luca breathed crushingly. 'Give me the car
keys.'

'The—?'

'You've had too much champagne.'

Darcy had had only a single glass. But out of guilt over
her undiplomatic tongue, she handed over the keys. He
swung into the driver's seat.

'You'll need directions.'

'I have total recall of our death-defying journey here.'

She let that comment on her driving ability go unchal-
lenged. She did drive pretty fast. And in three days' time
they needed to get married. There was now some source of
relief in the awareness that the marriage would be a fake.
He had no sense of humour and a filthy temper. Even
worse, he brooded. She stole a covert glance at his hard,
dark chiselled profile...but, gosh, he *still* looked spectacular!

In the moonlight, she averted her attention from him, torn
with shame at that betraying response. Deep in the pit of
her taut belly, she felt a surge of guilty heat, and was appalled by the immediacy of that reaction. He reminded her
of Zia's father...was that the problem? She shook her head
and studied her tightly linked hands, but although she tried
to fight off those painful memories, they began flooding
back...

When Richard had changed his mind about marrying her
three years earlier, Darcy had ended up taking their honeymoon trip solo. Of course it had been dismal. Blind to
the glorious sights, she had wandered round Venice as if
she was homeless, while she struggled to cope with the pain
of Richard's rejection. Then, one morning, she had witnessed a pair of youthful lovers having a stand-up row in
the Piazza San Marco. The sultry brunette had flung something at her boyfriend. As the thick gilded card had fluttered
to rest at Darcy's feet the fiery lovers had stalked off in

opposite directions. And Darcy had found herself in unexpected possession of an invite to a masked ball at one of
the wonderful palaces on the Grand Canal.

Two days later, she had finally rebelled against her bore-
dom and her loneliness. She had purchased a mask and had
donned that magical green evening dress. She had felt transformed, excitingly different and feminine. In those days she
hadn't owned contact lenses, and since her spectacles combined with her long mane of hair had seemed to give her
the dowdy look of an earnest swot she had taken them off,
choosing to embrace myopia instead. She had had a cold
too, so she had generously dosed herself up with a cold
remedy. Unfortunately she hadn't read the warning on the
packaging not to take any alcohol with the medication...

When she had seen the vast *palazzo* ablaze with golden
light she had almost lost her nerve, but a crush of important
guests had arrived at the same time, forcing her to move
ahead of them and pass over her invitation. She had
climbed the vast sweeping staircase of gilded brass and
marble. By the time she'd entered the superb mirrored ballroom, filled with exquisitely dressed crowds of beautiful
people awash with glittering jewels, her nerve had been
failing fast. At any minute she had feared exposure as a
gatecrasher, sneaking in where she had no right to be.

After hovering, trying desperately hard not to look con-
spicuous in her solitary state, she had slowly edged her path
round to the fluttering curtains on the far side of the huge
room and slid through them to find herself out on a big
stone balcony. One secure step removed from the festivi-
ties, she had watched the glamorous guests mingle and
dance—or at least she had watched them as closely as her
shortsightedness allowed.

When an unmasked male figure in a white jacket had
strolled out onto the balcony with a tray bearing a single
glass, to address her in Italian, she'd quite naturally assumed he was a waiter.

'*Grazie,*' she said, striving to appear as if she was just

taking the air after a dance or two, and draining the glass with appropriate thirsty fervour.

But he spoke again.

'I don't speak Italian—'

'That was Spanish,' he imparted gently in English. 'I thought you might be Spanish. That dress worn with such vibrant colouring as yours is dramatic.'

In the lingering silence of her disinterested shrug, he remarked, 'You appear to be alone.' Not easily disconcerted, he lounged lazily back against the stone balustrade, the tray abandoned.

'I *was*,' she pointed out thinly. 'And I like being alone.'

He inclined his dark head back, his features a complete blur at that distance, only his pale jacket clearly visible to her in the darkness as he stared at her. In a bolshy mood, she stared back, nose in the air, head imperiously high. All of a sudden she was sick to death of being pushed around by people and forced to fulfil *their* expectations. Her solo trip to Venice had been her first true rebellion, and so far she could not comfort herself with the belief that she had done much with the opportunity.

'You're prickly.'

'No, that was *rude*,' Darcy contradicted ruefully. 'Outright, bloody rudeness.'

'Is that an apology?' he enquired.

'No, I believe I was clarifying my point. And haven't you got any more drinks to ferry around?' she prompted hopefully.

He stilled, wide shoulders tautening, and then unexpectedly he laughed, a shiveringly sensual sound that sent a curious ripple down her taut spine. 'Not at present.'

His easy humour shamed her into a blush. 'I'm not in a very good mood.'

'I will change that.'

'Not could, but *will*,' she noted out loud. 'You're very sure of yourself.'

'Aren't you?'

In that instant, her own sheer lack of self-confidence flailed her with shamed bitterness, and she threw her head back with desperate pride and a tiny smile of wry amusement. 'Always,' she murmured steadily then. *'Always.'*

He moved forward, and as an arrow of light from the great chandeliers in the ballroom fell on him she saw an indistinct image of the hard, bitingly attractive angles of his strong bone structure, the gleam of his thick black hair, the brilliance of his dark eyes. And her heart skipped a startled beat.

'Dance with me,' he urged softly.

And Darcy laughed with undeniable appreciation. Only she could gatecrash a high society ball and end up being chatted up by one of the waiters. 'Aren't you scared that someone will see you and you'll lose your job?'

'Not if we remain out here...'

'Just one dance and then I'll leave.'

'The entertainment doesn't meet with your approval?' he probed as he slid her into his arms, his entire approach so subtle, so smooth that she was surprised to find herself there, and then flattered by the sensation of being held as if she were fashioned of the most fragile and delicate spun glass.

'It's suffocatingly formal, and tonight I feel like something different,' she mused with perfect truth. 'Indeed, tonight I feel just a little wild...'

'Please don't let me inhibit you,' he murmured.

And Darcy burst out laughing again.

'Who did you come here with tonight?' he queried.

'Nobody...I'm a gatecrasher,' she confided daringly.

'A *gatecrasher?*'

'You sound shocked...'

'Security is usually very tight at the Palazzo d'Oro.'

'Not if you enter just in front of a party who require a great deal of attentive bowing and scraping.'

'You must've had an invitation?'

'It landed at my feet in the Piazza San Marco. A beautiful

brunette flung it at her boyfriend. I thought you asked me to dance,' she complained, since they had yet to move. 'Are you now planning to have me thrown out?'

'Not just at present,' he confided, folding her closer and staring down at her with narrowed eyes. 'You are a very unusual woman.'

'Very,' Darcy agreed, liking that tag, which hinted at a certain distinction.

'And your name?'

'No names, no pack drill,' she sighed. 'Ships that pass and all that—'

'I want to board…'

'No can do. I am not my name…my name wasn't even chosen with me in mind,' she admitted with repressed bitterness, for Darcy had always been a male name in her family. 'And I want to be someone else tonight.'

'Very unusual and *very* infuriating,' he breathed.

'I am a woman who is very, very sure of herself, and a woman of that stature is certain to infuriate,' she returned playfully, leaning in to his big powerful body and smiling up at him, set free by anonymity to be whatever she wanted to be.

And so they danced, high above the Grand Canal, all the lights glittering magically in her eyes until she closed them and just drifted in a wonderful dreamy haze…

# CHAPTER FOUR

A BURST of forceful Italian dredged Darcy out of that sleepy, seductive flow of memory. Eyelids fluttering, she returned to the present and frowned to find the Land Rover at a standstill, headlights glaring on the high banks of a narrow lane.

'What...*where*—?' she began in complete confusion.

'We have a flat tyre,' Luca delivered in a murderous aside as he wrenched open the rattling driver's door.

Darcy scrambled out into the drizzling rain. 'But the spare's in for repair!' she exclaimed.

Across the bonnet, Luca surveyed her with what struck her as an overplay of all-male incredulity. 'You have *no* spare tyre?'

'No.' Darcy busied herself giving the offending flat tyre a kick. 'Pretty far gone, isn't it? That won't get us home.' She looked around herself. 'Where on earth *are* we?'

'It is possible that in the darkness I may have taken a wrong turn.'

Considering that they were in a lane that came to a dead end at a field twenty feet ahead, Darcy judged that a miracle of understatement. 'You got lost, didn't you?'

Luca dealt her a slaughtering, silencing glance.

Darcy sighed. 'We'd better start walking—'

'*Walking?*' He was aghast at the concept.

'What else? How long is it since you saw a main road?'

'Some time,' Luca gritted. 'But fortunately there is a farmhouse quite close.'

'Fat lot of use that's going to be,' Darcy muttered. 'At two in the morning, only an emergency would give us the excuse to knock people up out of their beds.'

'This *is* an emergency!'

Darcy drew herself up to her full five feet two inches. 'I am not rousing an entire family just so that we can ask to use their phone. In any case, who would you suggest I contact?'

'A motoring organisation,' Luca informed her with ex-aggerated patience.

'I don't belong to one.'

'A car breakdown recovery business?'

'Have you any idea what that would cost?' Darcy groaned in horror. 'It's not worth it for a flat tyre! The local garage can run out the spare in the morning. They'll only charge me for their time and petrol—'

'I am not spending the night in that filthy vehicle,' Luca asserted levelly.

'You figure cosying up to those cows would be more fun?' Darcy could not resist saying, surveying the curious beasts who, attracted by the light and the sound of their voices, had ambled up to gawk over the gate at them.

'I passed through a crossroads about a kilometre back. I saw an inn there.' With the decisive air of one taking command, Luca leant into the car. 'I presume you have a torch?'

''Fraid not,' Darcy admitted gruffly.

Not a male who took life's little slings and arrows with a stiff upper lip, Darcy registered by the stark exhalation of breath. Not remotely like the charming, tolerant male she had encountered in Venice three years ago. And how the heck she had contrived to imagine the faintest resemblance now quite escaped her. This was a male impatient of any mishap which injured his comfort—indeed, almost outraged by any set of circumstances which could strand him ignominiously on a horribly wet night in a muddy country lane.

So they walked.

'I should have paid some heed to where we were going,' Darcy remarked, proffering a generous olive branch.

'''If onlys'' exasperate me,' Luca divulged.

Rain trickling down her bare arms, Darcy buttoned her lips. With a stifled imprecation, Luca removed his dinner jacket and held it out to her.

'Oh, don't be daft,' Darcy muttered in astonished embarrassment at such a gesture. 'I'm as tough as old boots.'

'I *insist*—'

'No...no, honestly.' Darcy started walking again in haste. 'You've just come from a hot climate...you're more at risk of a chill than I am.'

*'Per amor di Dio...'* Luca draped the jacket round her narrow shoulders, enfolding her in the smooth silk lining which still carried the pervasive heat and scent of his body. 'Just keep quiet and wear it!'

In the darkness, a spontaneous grin of appreciation lit Darcy's face. As she stumbled on the rough road surface Luca curved a steadying arm round her, and instead of withdrawing that support, kept it there. It was amazing how good that made her feel. He had tremendously good manners, she conceded. Not unnaturally, he was infuriated by the inefficiency that had led to the absence of a spare tyre, but at least he wasn't doggedly set on continually reminding her of her oversight.

The inn perched at the juncture of lanes was shrouded in darkness. Darcy hung back in the porch. 'Do we *have* to do this?'

Without a shade of hesitation, Luca strode forward to make use of the ornate door-knocker. 'I would knock up the dead for a brandy and a hot bath.'

An outside light went on. A bleary-eyed middle-aged man in a dressing gown eventually appeared. Darcy heard the rustle of money. The security chain was undone at speed. And suddenly mine host became positively convivial. Getting dragged out of his bed in the middle of the night might almost have been a pleasure to him. He showed them up a creaking, twisting staircase into a pleasant room and retreated to fetch the brandy.

'How much money did you give him, for heaven's sake?' Darcy demanded in fascination.

'Sufficient to cover the inconvenience.' Luca surveyed the room and the connecting bathroom with a frowning lack of appreciation.

'It's really quite cosy,' Darcy remarked, and it was when compared with her own rather barn-like and bare bedroom at the Folly. The floor had a carpet and the bed had a fat satin quilt.

The proprietor reappeared with an entire bottle of brandy and two glasses.

Darcy discarded the jacket, studying Luca, whose white shirt was plastered to an impressive torso which gleamed brown through the saturated fabric. Her attention fairly caught as she stood there, tousled hair dripping down her rainwashed face, she glimpsed the black whorls of hair hazing his muscular chest in a distinctive male triangle as he turned back to her. Her face burned.

'Give me a coin,' Darcy told him abruptly.

A curious brow quirking, Luca withdrew a coin from his pocket. 'What—?'

Darcy flipped it from his fingers. 'We'll toss for the bed.'

'I beg your pardon?'

But Darcy had already tossed. 'Heads or tails?' she proffered cheerfully.

'Dio—'

'Heads!' Darcy chose impatiently. She uncovered the coin and then sighed. 'You get the bed; I get the quilt. Do you mind if I have first shower? I'll be quick.'

Moving to the bathroom without awaiting a reply, Darcy closed the door with some satisfaction. The trick was to get over embarrassing ground fast. Had money not been in short supply, she would've asked for a second room, but why bother for the sake of a few hours? Luca was highly unlikely to succumb to an attack of overpowering lust and make a pass… I should be so lucky, she thought, and then squirmed with boiling guilt.

Stripping off, she stepped into the shower. In five minutes she was out again, smothering a yawn. After towel-drying her hair, she put her bra and pants back on, draped her sodden dress over one exact half of the shower curtain rail and opened the door a crack.

The room was empty. Darcy shot across the bedroom, snatched the quilt and a pillow off the divan, and in ten seconds flat had herself tucked in her makeshift bed on the carpet.

Ten minutes later, Luca reappeared. '*Accidenti*...this isn't a schoolgirl sleep-over!' he bit out, sounding as if he was climbing the walls with exasperation. 'We'll share the bed like grown-ups.'

'I'm perfectly happy where I am. I lost the toss.'

Luca growled something raw and impatient in Italian.

'I've slept in far less comfortable places than this. Do stop fussing,' she muttered, her voice muffled by the quilt. 'I'm a lot hardier than you are—'

'And what is *that* supposed to mean?'

Her wide, anxious gaze appeared over the edge of the satin quilt. She collided with heartstopping dark golden eyes glittering with suspicion below flaring ebony brows. Her stomach clenched, her breath shortening in her dry throat. 'Why don't you go and get your hot bath and your brandy?' she suggested tautly, and in so doing tactfully side-stepped the question.

Dear heaven, but he was gorgeous. She listened to him undress. She wanted to look. As the bathroom door closed on him she grimaced, feverishly hot and uneasy and thoroughly ashamed of herself. He was a decent guy and he had made a real effort on her behalf tonight. A Hollywood film star couldn't have been more impressive in his role. And here she was, acting all silly like the schoolgirl he had hinted she was, reacting to him as if he was a sex object and absolutely nothing else. Didn't she despise men who regarded women in that light?

Sure, Darcy, when was the last time a male treated *you*

like a sex object? *Venice*. She shivered. Instantly she remembered that passionate kiss out on the balcony high above the Grand Canal, how that fierce sizzle of electric excitement in her veins had felt that very first time. Excitement as dangerously addictive as a narcotic drug. And tonight she had experienced that same wild hunger all over again...

A hot, liquid sensation assailing the very crux of her body, Darcy bit her lower lip and loathed her weak, wanton physical self. But no wonder she had been shaken up earlier. No wonder she had briefly imagined more than a superficial resemblance of looks and nationality between Luca and her daughter's father. But there *was* no mystery. Her own shatteringly powerful response to both men had been the sole source of similarity.

The bathroom door opened, heralding Luca's return.

'Darcy...get into the bed,' Luca instructed very drily.

Darcy ignored the invitation, terrified that he might sense her attraction to him if she got any closer. 'I never really thanked you properly for tonight,' she said instead, eager to change the subject. 'You were a class act.'

'*Grazie*...would you like a brandy?'

'No, thanks.'

After the chink of glass, she heard the blankets being trailed back, the creak as the divan gave under his weight. The light went out. 'You know, when I said you'd make a great gigolo, I was really trying to pay you a compliment,' she advanced warily.

'I'll bear that in mind.'

Emboldened by that apparent new tolerance, Darcy relaxed. 'I suppose I owe you an explanation about a few things...' In the darkness, she grimaced, but she felt that he had earned greater honesty. 'When I was a child, Fielding's Folly paid for itself. But Margo liked to live well and my father took out a mortgage rather than reduce their outgoings. I only found out about the mortgage a couple of years ago, when the Folly needed roof repairs and the estate couldn't afford to pay for them.'

'Wasn't your stepmother prepared to help?'

'No. In fact Margo tried to persuade my father to sell up. I was really scared she might wear him down,' she confided. 'That was when we had a bit of *good* luck for a change. I had a piece of antique jewellery valued and we ended up selling that instead—'

'A piece of jewellery?' Luca interposed with silken softness.

'A ring. My father had forgotten it even existed, but that ring fetched a really tidy sum,' Darcy shared with quiet pride.

'Fancy that,' Luca drawled, and the dark timbre of his deep-pitched accented voice slid down her spine in the most curiously enervating fashion. 'Did you sell it on the open market?'

In the darkness, Darcy turned over restively. 'No, it was a private sale. I assumed the estate was secure then. I didn't realise how serious things really were until my father died. He never confided in me. But you have to understand that there is nothing I wouldn't do to keep the Folly in the family.'

'I understand that perfectly.'

Darcy licked at her taut lower lip. 'So when my wealthy godmother died a few months ago, I was really hoping that she would leave me some money...'

'Nothing more natural,' Luca conceded encouragingly.

'There were three of us...three god-daughters. Myself, Maxie and Polly,' Darcy enumerated heavily. 'But when the will was read, we all got a shock. Nancy left us a share of her estate, but only on condition that we each marry within the year.'

'How extraordinary...'

'So that's why I needed you...to inherit.' The hardness of the floor was starting to make its presence felt through the layers of both carpet and quilt. Shifting from one slender unpadded hip to the other with increased discomfort, Darcy added uneasily, 'I suppose you think that's rather calculating and greedy of me...?'

'No, I think you are very brave to take me on trust,' Luca delivered gently.

Darcy smiled, relieved by the assurance and encouraged. 'This floor is kind of hard...' she admitted finally.

'And you're being such a jolly good sport about it,' Luca remarked slumberously from the comfort of the bed. 'I really admire that quality in a woman.'

'Do you?' Darcy whispered in surprise.

'But of course. You're so *delightfully* democratic! No feminine sulks or pleas for special treatment,' Luca pointed out approvingly. 'You lost the toss and you took it on the chin just like a man would.'

Darcy nodded slowly. 'I guess I did.'

It didn't seem quite the moment to suggest that he took the floor instead. But a helpless little kernel of inner warmth blossomed at his praise. He mightn't fancy her but he seemed to at least respect her.

'*Buona notte,* Darcy.'

'Goodnight, Luca.'


Darcy woke with a start to find Luca standing over her fully dressed. She blinked in confusion. He looked so impossibly tall, dark and handsome.

'The Land Rover's outside,' he imparted.

'Outside...*how?*' She sat up, hugging the quilt and striving not to wince as every aching muscle she possessed shrieked complaint.

'I called your local garage. They were keen to help. I'll see you downstairs for breakfast,' Luca concluded.

It was already after nine. Darcy hurried into the bathroom and looked in anguish at her reflection. Overnight her hair had exploded into dozens of babyish Titian curls. She ran her fingers through them and they all stood up on end. In despair, she tried to push them down again.

Ten minutes later, Darcy went downstairs, curls damped down, last night's dress crumpled, and the sensation of looking an absolute mess doing nothing for her confidence. She slunk over to the corner table where Luca was semi-concealed behind a newspaper, beautifully shaped dark imperious head bent, luxuriant black hair immaculate, not a single strand out of place.

Darcy sank down opposite, in no hurry to draw attention to herself. And then her attention fell on the photograph of the statuesque blonde adorning the front page of his newspaper. 'Give me that paper!' she gasped. *'Please!'*

Ebony brows knitting in incomprehension, Luca began lowering the paper, but Darcy reached over and snatched it from him without further ado, spreading the publication flat on the table to read the blurb that went with the picture.

'She's married already…*married!*' Darcy groaned in appalled disbelief. 'Page four…' she muttered, frantically leafing through the pages to reach the main story.

'Who has got married?'

'Maxie Kendall…one of Nancy's other god-daughters.'

'The lady has beaten you to the finishing line?' Luca enquired smoothly.

Darcy was too busy reading to reply. 'Angelos Petronides…oh, dear heaven would you look at that dirty great enormous mansion they're standing outside?' she demanded in stricken appeal. 'Not only has she got herself a husband, he looks *besotted,* and he *has* to be loaded—'

'Angelos Petronides…yes…loaded,' Luca confirmed very drily.

'I feel *ill!*' Darcy confessed truthfully, thrusting the offending newspaper away in disgust.

'Jealous…envious?'

Darcy turned shaken eyes of reproach on him. 'Oh, no…it's just…it's just everything always seems so *easy* for Maxie…she's incredibly beautiful! We were practically best friends until Richard fell in love with her. That's why we didn't get married,' she completed tightly.

After that dialogue, breakfast was a silent meal. Darcy was embarrassed by her outburst and insulted by his response. Jealous? Envious? She thought about that as she drove them back to the Folly. *No*...Luca had got her completely wrong.

As her chief bridesmaid, Maxie had stayed at the Folly the week running up to that misfired wedding three years earlier. The glamorous model had accepted the bridegroom's attention and admiration as her due, responding with flirtatious smiles and amusing repartee. Richard had been, quite simply, *dazzled*. And Darcy had been naively pleased that her friend and her fiancé appeared to be getting on so well.

But on their wedding day Richard had turned to look at Darcy at the altar, only to confess in despair, 'I *can't* go through with this...'

The wedding party had adjourned to the vestry.

'I've fallen in love with Maxie,' Richard had admitted baldly, his shame and distress at having to make that admission unconcealed.

'What the hell are you talking about?' Maxie had demanded furiously. 'I don't even *like* you!'

Fierce anger had filled Darcy then. She could have borne that devastating change of heart better had Maxie returned Richard's feelings. Then, at least, there might have seemed some point to the whole ghastly mess. But Maxie's careless encouragement of male homage had done the damage. Both Darcy *and* Richard had been bitterly hurt and humiliated by the experience.

Darcy had long since forgiven Richard, indeed still regarded him as a dear friend. Yet she had not been half so generous to Maxie, she conceded now. She had awarded her former friend the lion's share of the blame. Only now did it occur to her that Maxie had been a thoughtless teenager at the time, she herself only a year older. Perhaps, she reflected grudgingly, she had been unjust...

Face still and strained over her troubling reflections, for

Darcy never liked to think that she had been less than fair, she climbed out of the Land Rover outside the Folly.

'Do you realise that you have not spoken a single word since breakfast?' Luca enquired without any expression at all.

Darcy tautened defensively. 'I was thinking about Richard.'

Dark colour slowly rose to accentuate the hard angles of Luca's slashing cheekbones, his lean, strong face tightening. He surveyed her from beneath dense inky black lashes, eyes broodingly dark and icy cold. Colliding unexpectedly with that chilling scrutiny, Darcy felt her stomach clench as if she had hit black ice. 'What's wrong?'

'What could possibly be wrong?'

'I don't know, but...' Darcy continued with a frown of uncertainty. 'Gosh, I owe you some money for our overnight stay—'

'I will present you with a bill for all services rendered,' Luca asserted with sardonic cool.

'Thanks...a cheque might bounce if I wrote it today.' But Darcy's green eyes remained anxious. 'When are you planning to move in?' she asked abruptly.

'The day of our wedding,' Luca revealed.

'So what time will you be here, then?' she pressed.

'I'll be at the church in time for the ceremony.' An almost dangerous smile curved his wide, sensual mouth. 'You need cherish no fear that I might fail to show. After all, in this materialistic world, you get what you pay for.'

Disturbed at having her secret apprehensions so easily read, Darcy watched him stroll fluidly towards the Porsche. How did he do it? she wondered then in fierce frustration. How *did* he contrive to make her agonisingly aware of that dynamic masculinity and virile sexuality even as he walked away from her? The angle of his proud dark head, the strong set of his wide shoulders, the sleek twist of his lean hips and the indolent grace of those long, powerful legs as he moved all grabbed and held her attention.

As he opened the car door he glanced back at her.

Caught staring again, Darcy looked as guilty as she felt.

'By the way,' Luca murmured silkily, 'I forgot to mention how impressed I was by that pre-nuptial contract I signed. That we each leave the marriage with exactly what we brought into it is very fair.'

'Sexual equality,' Darcy muttered, unable to take her eyes off the way the sunlight glistened over black hair she already knew felt like luxurious silk beneath her fingertips. And she recalled with a little frisson of helpless pleasure how good it had felt in Margo and Nina's radius to have a man by her side she could trust.

'I'm *all* for it,' Luca informed her lazily, angling the most shatteringly sensual smile of approval at her.

Even at a distance that fascinating smile had the power to jolt and send a current of all too warm appreciation quivering through her. As he drove off, Darcy gave him a jerky, self-conscious wave.


'Do you realise how often you have mentioned Luca's name over the past two days?' Karen prompted tautly.

'Luca *is* rather central to my plans, and we are getting married tomorrow,' Darcy pointed out with some amusement as she straightened Zia's bed, Karen having arrived in the midst of the bedtime story ritual. 'Love you, sweetheart,' she whispered, dropping a kiss on her daughter's smooth brow.

The toddler mumbled a sleepy response and burrowed below the duvet until only a cluster of black curls showed. Darcy switched off the bedside light and walked out into the corridor, leaving the door ajar.

'I'm scared that you're developing a crush on the guy,' Karen delivered baldly, determined to send the message of her concern fully home.

'I think I'm a little too mature for a crush, Karen—'

'That's what's worrying me.' The brunette grimaced. 'You are *paying* Luca to put on a good act. He's hired help—whatever you want to call it… You can't afford to fall in love with him!'

Darcy looked pained. 'I'm not going to fall in love with him.'

'Then why do you keep on talking about how much he shone at Margo's party?'

'Because I give honour where it's due and he *did!*'

'Not to mention how wonderful his manners are and how many and varied are the subjects on which he can converse like Einstein!' Karen completed doggedly.

'So I was impressed…' Darcy shrugged, but her cheeks were flushed, her eyes evasive.

'Darcy…you've had a pretty rough time the last couple of years and you're vulnerable,' Karen spelt out uncomfortably. 'I'm sure Luca is a really terrific bloke, but you don't know him well enough to trust him yet. In fact, he could be thinking you'll be a darned good catch with this house behind you.'

'He knows I'm in debt up to my eyeballs,' Darcy contradicted.

Confronted with the full extent of her friend's unease, however, Darcy took some time to get to sleep that night. Was it so obvious that she was attracted to Luca? Was it obvious to *him?* She cringed at the suspicion. But, even so, Karen was mad to suggest that she was in danger of falling for Luca.

She had returned from Venice with a heart broken into so many pieces she had been torn apart by her own turmoil. Falling like a ton of bricks for a complete stranger in the space of one night had been a hard lesson indeed. Her battered pride, her pain and her despair had taken a very long time to fade. Darcy had not the slightest intention of allowing her undeniable attraction to Luca go one step further than appreciation from a safe distance.

In its day, it had been a costly designer dress. The ivory silk wedding gown hugged Darcy's shoulders, smoothly

clung to her slender waist and hips and fanned out into
beautifully embroidered panels between mid-thigh and ankle. It had belonged to her late mother, and, foolish and
uneasy as she felt at using the dress for such a purpose, she
thought it would look very odd if she didn't make some
effort to put on a show of being a *real* bride.

And this afternoon Darcy also had an important appointment to keep with her bank manager. Hopefully a candid
explanation of the terms of her godmother's will would
persuade the older man that the Folly was a more secure
investment than he had previously believed. With his agreement she would be able to re-employ the most vital estate
workers, and very soon things would get back to normal
around her home, she thought cheerfully.

'Pretty Mummy,' Zia enthused, liquid dark eyes huge as
she took an excited twirl in the pink summer dress and frilly
ankle socks which she loved. 'Pretty Zia?' she added.

'*Very* pretty,' Darcy agreed with a grin.

Karen drove them to the church in her car. Darcy was
shaken to see quite a crowd waiting in the churchyard to
see her arrive. She recognised every face. Former estate
staff and tenants, people she had known all her life.

An older woman who had retired as the Folly's last
housekeeper moved forward to press a beautiful bouquet
into Darcy's empty hands. 'Everybody's so happy for you,
Miss Fielding,' she said with embarrassing fervour. 'We all
hope you have a *really* wonderful day!'

As other voices surged to offer the same sincere good
wishes for her future happiness, Darcy's eyes stung and
flooded with rare tears. She blinked rapidly, touched to the
heart but also wrenched by guilt that her coming marriage
would only be an empty pretence.

As she entered the small church, Luca turned his imperious head to stare down the aisle. His strong, dark face
stilled in what might have been surprise at her appearance
in the silk gown, dark golden eyes glittering. Darcy's tear-
drenched gaze ran over him. Sheathed in an exquisitely

tailored charcoal-grey suit, he exuded the most breathtaking aura of command and sophistication. He had such incredible impact that she forgot how to breathe and her knees wobbled. There was just *something* about him, she thought with dizzy discomfiture.

Unexpectedly, another, younger man stood beside Luca. Slim and dark, he looked tense, his eyes slewing away from Darcy as she gave him a friendly nod of acknowledgement.

The ceremony began. Only at the point where Luca took her hand to put on the ring did Darcy register that she had totally overlooked the necessity of supplying one. Relief filled her when Luca produced a narrow gold band and slid it onto her wedding finger. 'Thanks…' she muttered, only half under her breath, reddening at the vicar's look of surprise at that unusual bridal reaction.

When the brief marriage service was concluded, the register was signed. Karen and the other man, whom Luca addressed as Benito, performed their function as witnesses. All formalities dealt with, Darcy rubbed her still damp and stinging eyes, and accidentally dislodged one of her contact lenses. With an exclamation of dismay, she dropped to her knees. 'Don't move, anyone…I've lost one of my lenses!'

Luca reached down and flicked up the tiny item from where it glimmered on the stone floor. He slipped it into his pocket, evidently aware that without the aid of cleansing solution she could not immediately replace the lens. 'Relax, I have it…'

Amazed by the speed of his reactions, Darcy skimmed a glance up at him. At the same time he bent down to help her upright again. As she focused myopically on him through one eye, she closed the other in an involuntary attempt to see better. In that split second his features blurred, throwing his strong facial bones into a different kind of prominence that lent them a stark, haunting familiarity. Darcy froze in outright disbelief. Her Venetian lover!

In that instant of incredulous recognition shock seized

her by the throat and almost strangled the life force from her. 'You...*y-you?*' she began, stammering wildly.

Darcy gaped at Luca in an uncomprehending stupor. Her head pounded sickly and he swam back out of focus again. As she blacked out, Luca caught her in his arms before she could fall.

# CHAPTER FIVE

'TAKE a deep breath…' Luca's deep, dark drawl instructed with complete calm.

Whoosh. The air flooded back into Darcy's constricted lungs. Perspiration broke out on her clammy brow. Her eyes fluttered open again. She found herself seated on a hard wooden pew.

'*See…*' Karen was soothing Zia, several feet away. 'Mummy's all right.' And then, in a whispered aside to Luca, 'I bet Darcy fainted because she's exhausted—she works eighteen-hour days!'

As Darcy lifted her swimming head everything came hurtling back to her. She simply gawped at Luca, still doubting the stunning evidence provided by that one myopic glance. Shimmering dark eyes held her bemused gaze steadily, and all over again that frantically disorientating sense of frightening familiarity gripped her.

'You can't be…you *can't* be!' she gasped abruptly, impervious to the presence of the others.

'Take it easy, Darcy,' Karen advised, evidently unaware that anything was seriously wrong. 'You passed out and you're confused, that's all. Look, I'll keep Zia with me until you're feeling better. You should lie down for a while. I'll call over later and see how you are.'

Still in a world of her own, Darcy moved her muzzy head as if she was afraid it might fall off her neck. Luca Raffacani could not be the man with whom she had spent the night in Venice; he could not *possibly* be the same man! And yet, he *was!* It made no sense, it seemed beyond the bounds of even the wildest feat of imagination, but those

74

strong promptings of familiarity which had troubled her apparently had their basis in solid fact.

'Can you stand?' Luca enquired.

'I'm fine...really,' Darcy whispered unconvincingly as she fought to focus her mind. She got up on legs that felt like cotton wool sticks. She shook hands with the vicar, who was anxiously hovering. Then she stared at Luca again with a kind of appalled fascination and knew she would never feel fine again, knew she felt, rather, as if she had lost her mind in that devastating moment of recognition.

'The car's outside, sir.' Benito spoke for the first time as he turned from the window.

Darcy's attention swivelled to the younger man. *Sir?* She encountered a fleeting look of pity in Benito's gaze. The sort of pity one experienced for someone sick when all hope had gone, Darcy labelled with a bemused shudder.

What on earth was going on? Who *was* Gianluca Fabrizio Raffacani? And whoever he was, whatever he was, she had just made him her husband!

'Calm yourself,' Luca urged before they walked back out of the church to face the crowd of well-wishers waiting to see them off.

'But I recognised you...' she told him shakily.

'You mean you *finally* shuffled the memory of one face out of the no doubt countless one-night stands you have enjoyed?' Luca murmured in a silken smooth stab, making her shrink in stricken disbelief at such a charge. 'Am I to feel honoured by that most belated distinction?'

His cool confirmation that he was who she believed he was shook Darcy up even more. In the back of her mind she had still somehow expected and foolishly hoped that Luca would turn with a raised brow to tell her that he hadn't a clue what she was talking about.

'You don't understand,' she began, in an unsteady attempt to defend herself, so confused was she still. 'I could hardly see you that night, not in any detail...your face was a blur and out of focus—you looked different...'

'I guess one bird for the plucking looks much like another,' Luca responded with a sardonic bite that sizzled
down her spine like a hurricane warning and made her turn
even paler.

A bird for the plucking? She didn't understand that crack
any more than she could understand anything else. As they
left the churchyard her attention fell on the big silver limousine waiting by the kerb. Pressed into a vehicle which
was the very last word in expensive luxury, she was even
more bewildered. Benito swung into the front seat. The
tinted glass barrier between the front and the back of the
limo was partially open, denying them privacy.

Darcy snatched in a shuddering breath. Her brain ached,
all at once throwing up a dozen even more confusing in-
consistencies. In a daze, she struggled hopelessly to super-
impose the image of the Luca she had thought she was
getting to know over her memory of the male who had
romanced her in Venice, the sleek, seductive rat who had
torn her inside out with the pain of loss…

Involuntarily she focused on Luca again. There was a
strikingly relaxed quality to the indolent sprawl of his
strong, supple body. In the state Darcy was in, that supreme
poise and cool was uniquely intimidating.

Within minutes the limo drew up outside the Folly.
Darcy scrambled out in haste, her heartbeat banging in her
eardrums. With damp, nerveless hands she unlocked and
thrust open the heavy front door to walk into the echoing
medieval hall with its aged flagstoned floor.

She spun round, then, to face Luca, where he had stilled
by the giant smoke-blackened stone fireplace. Her oval face
was stiff with strain as she attempted to match his aura of
complete self-command.

'I can't believe that coincidence has anything to do with
this…' Darcy admitted jaggedly.

'Very wise.' Luca surveyed her with a grim satisfaction
that was chilling.

'How could you *possibly* have found out who I was…or where I lived?'

'With persistence, no problem is insuperable. It took time, but I had you traced.'

'You had me traced…dear heaven, *why?*' Darcy could not hide her incredulity. 'Why the heck would you even want to do such a thing?'

'Don't play dumb,' Luca advised with derision.

Darcy shook her head dizzily as she braced her hands on the back of a tapestry-covered chair to steady herself. 'You came to that interview in disguise…you have to be certifiably nuts to have gone to such outrageous lengths—'

'No…merely guilty of the inexpressibly vain assumption that I might be in some danger of being recognised.'

Darcy winced at that jibe and closed her eyes, but then she had to open them again, possessed as she was by a sick compulsion to keep on watching Luca. But his lean, hard features betrayed nothing. 'Why did you *do* this? What's in it for you? You can't be unemployed or b-broke.'

'No… What was that vulgar term you used about your fortunate friend, Maxie? I'm "loaded",' Luca conceded with a scornful twist of his lips. 'But you will not profit from that reality, I assure you.'

'I don't understand…' Her hand flew up to her pounding temples. 'I'm getting the most awful headache.'

'Retribution hurts,' Luca slotted in softly. 'And by the time I am finished with you, a headache will be the very least of your problems.'

'What's that supposed to mean? For heaven's sake…are you *threatening* me?' Darcy gasped, releasing her hold on the chair to take an angry step forward.

'No, I believe I am revelling in the extraordinary sense of power I'm experiencing. I've never felt like that around a woman before,' Luca mused thoughtfully. 'But then, where you are concerned, I have no pity.'

'You're trying to scare me…'

'How easily do you scare?' Luca enquired with appalling self-possession.

'You don't behave like the man I met in Venice!' Darcy condemned shakily.

'You're not the woman I met then either. But she'll emerge eventually... I have this wonderful conviction that over the next six months whatever I want, I will receive.' Brilliant dark eyes gleamed with cruel amusement below level black brows. 'My every wish will be your command. *Nothing* will be too much trouble. I will just snap my fingers and you will jump...'

Darcy tried and failed to swallow. The living nightmare of her own confusion was growing. While one small part of her stood back and believed that he was talking outrageous nonsense, all the rest of her was horribly impressed by the lethal edge of cool, collected threat in that rich, dark drawl and the deadly chill in his level gaze. 'What are you trying to say?'

'As a sobering taste of your near future, consider this...depending on my choice of timing, if I walk out on this marriage *you* will lose *everything* you possess.' Luca spelt out that reminder with an immovable cool that made what he was saying all the more shocking.

The silence, broken only by the steady tick of the grandfather clock, hung there between them as breakable as a thin sheet of glass.

'No...no...' Every scrap of remaining colour drained from Darcy's shaken face as she absorbed the full weight of that threat. 'You *can't* do that to me!'

'I think you'll find that I can do anything I want...' Strolling closer with fluid ease, Luca stretched out a seemingly idle hand and closed it over her clenched fingers. Slowly, relentlessly employing the pressure of his infinitely greater strength, he pulled her towards him.

'Stop it...let go of me!' Darcy cried, totally unprepared for this even more daunting development, heartbeat thundering in panic, breath snarling up in her convulsing throat.

'That is no way to talk to a new husband,' Luca censured indolently as he skimmed a confident hand down to the shallow indentation at the base of her spine and held her there, mere inches from him. He studied her with satisfaction. 'And particularly not one with such *high* expectations of your future behaviour. All that cutesy tossing of coins and sleeping on the floor like a naive little virgin…it's *wasted* on a male who has perfect recall of being pushed down on a bed and having his shirt ripped off within hours of meeting you!'

As that rich, dark-timbred voice flailed down her taut spine like a silken whip, Darcy's eyes grew huge and raw with stricken recollection of her own abandon that night in Venice. She trembled, her pallor now laced with hot ribbons of pink.

'You were *wild*,' Luca savoured huskily. 'It may be the most expensive one-night stand I ever had, but the sex was unforgettable.'

*Expensive?* But she still couldn't concentrate. She gazed up at him, as trapped as a butterfly speared by a cruel pin. Only in her case the pin was the stabbing thrust of intense humiliation piercing her to the heart. Raising one lean brown hand, he rubbed a blunt forefinger over the tremulous line of her full lower lip and she shivered, spooked by the blaze of those brilliant dark golden eyes so close, the shocking effect of that insolent caress on her tender mouth. With stunned disconcertion she felt a spark of heat flame into a smouldering tight little knot that scorched the pit of her tense stomach.

'You burned me alive,' Luca whispered mesmerically. 'And you're going to do that for me again…and again…and again until I don't want you any more…is that understood?'

No, nothing was understood. Too much had happened too fast, and at absolutely the wrong psychological moment. Darcy had stood at that altar, firmly and exultantly believing that she was in the very act of solving her every problem. Everything had fallen apart when she was least equipped to deal with it. Now she was simply reeling from moment to moment in the suffocating grip of deep, paralysing shock.

'Who *are* you...why are you doing this to me?' she demanded all over again, her incomprehension unconcealed as he released her.

'Isn't it strange how the passage of time operates?' Luca remarked with a philosophical air. 'What you once didn't want to know for your own protection, you are now desperate to discover—'

'You can't do this to me...you can't threaten me...I won't *let* you!' Darcy swore vehemently.

'Watch me,' Luca advised, consulting the rapier-thin gold watch on his wrist with tremendous poise. 'Now, I suggest you locate your passport and start packing.'

'Passport...*p-packing?*' Darcy parroted.

'My surprise, *cara.*' His mocking smile didn't add one iota of warmth to the cold brilliance of his dark eyes. 'In a couple of hours a helicopter will pick us up and take us to the airport. We're flying to Venice. I want to go home.'

Darcy backed away from him, green eyes burnished by angry bewilderment. 'Venice? Are you out of your mind? I'm not going to Italy with you!'

A fleeting smile of sardonic amusement curved his expressive mouth. 'Think that refusal through. If I leave this house without you, I will not return, and you will forfeit any hope of winning your inheritance in six months' time.'

'You bastard...' Darcy mumbled sickly as that message sank in. Evidently Luca knew far more than she had naively told him. He knew the *exact* conditions of her godmother's will. A marriage that lasted less than that six-month deadline would not count.

His stunning dark eyes narrowed to an icy splinter of gold. 'In the light of the circumstances of your child's birth, I'm astonished to hear you use that particular word.'

Slashed with guilty unease by that unwelcome reminder,

Darcy's facial muscles locked tight. *Zia*...her mind screamed with equal suddenness, as she finally faced up to and acknowledged the connection between this particular male and her child. *Their* child. The furious colour in her cheeks receded to leave her pale as milk. Zia was Luca's daughter as well—not that he appeared to have even a suspicion of the fact, although he seemed to have a daunting grasp of every other confidential aspect of her life.

'And by the way,' Luca murmured *sotto voce,* 'when you collect your daughter from the lodge, try not to forget the confidentiality clause in the pre-nuptial contract we both signed. If you talk about this, I will talk to the executor of your godmother's will.'

Darcy closed her eyes tightly again. 'I can't believe this is happening to me...' she ground out unsteadily.

And it was true. She had played into his hands so completely that she had tied herself in knots. Her home, her security, both her future and her daughter's were entirely reliant on Luca maintaining his verbal agreement with her. If they parted company a day before that six months was up, she would indeed lose everything she had worked so hard to retain.

Luca lifted one of her hands and lazily uncurled her fingers to plant something into her palm. 'Your missing lens...perhaps if you replace it, your view of the world will be clarified.'

Her lashes flew up. 'You are one sarcastic—!'

'And when you have shed the equivalent of Miss Havisham's wedding gown, which strangely enough does more for you than anything I have recently seen you in, is it possible that you could dig very deep into your wardrobe and produce something even passably presentable in which to travel?' Luca enquired gently.

'I'm not going to Italy...I'm not leaving to go *anywhere*...I have too many responsibilities here!' Darcy shot at him in a rising crescendo of desperation. 'This is my home...you cannot make me leave it!'

'I can't *make* you do anything,' Luca conceded softly. 'The choice is yours.'

Outrage gripped Darcy at that quip. Both her hands closed into fierce fists of frustration. 'You're blackmailing me…what choice do I have?'

Luca surveyed her with immovable cool and said nothing.

Unnerved by that lack of reaction, Darcy twisted away and raced upstairs to her bedroom.

Her mind was in a state of utter turmoil, stray thoughts hitting her like thrown knives thudding into a shrinking target. How would Luca feel if he found out that she had conceived his child that night in Venice? She was in no hurry to find out. Wouldn't that give him even more power over her? And why the heck had she had Zia christened Venezia? Or was that fanciful use of the Italian name of that great city too remote a connection to occur to anyone but her own foolish and sentimental self?

What the heck was Luca trying to do to her? Most of all, her brain screeched, *why* was he doing it? His behaviour made not the smallest sense. In fact her sheer inability to comprehend why Luca Raffacani should have employed diabolical cunning and deception to sneak into her life and threaten to blow it asunder was the most terrifying aspect of all. He knew so much about her, but as yet she knew next to nothing about him—and ignorance was not bliss!

Galvanised into action by that acknowledgement, Darcy reached for the phone by her bed and punched out the number of Richard's stud farm, praying he was in his office because he hated mobile phones and refused to carry one. 'Richard…it's Darcy—'

'How are you, old girl?' Richard cut in warmly. 'Odd you should ring. I was actually thinking of dropping down this—'

'Richard…do you remember telling me that it's possible to find almost any information you want on the Internet?'

Darcy interrupted with scant ceremony. 'Could you do that for me as a favour and fax anything you get?'

'Sure. What kind of information are you after?'

'Anything you can get on an Italian called…Gianluca Raffacani.'

'There's something vaguely familiar about that surname,' Richard commented absently. 'I wonder if he's into horses…'

'I'll be grateful for anything you can send me, but don't tell anyone I've been enquiring,' she warned nervously.

'No problem. Anything wrong down there?' he enquired. 'You sound harassed. What's the connection? Who is this chap?'

'That's what I'm trying to find out. Talk to you soon…thanks, Richard.' Darcy replaced the receiver.

She studied the framed photo of Richard by her bed and gave his grinning cheerful image the thumbs-up sign. To fight Luca she had to find out who and what she was dealing with.

No way could she go to Italy! The Folly could not be left empty. And who would feed the hens and Nero, her elderly horse, look after the dogs? Work that the wedding had so far prevented her from carrying out today, she recalled dully. Shedding her late mother's gown, she pulled on her work jeans and an old sweater. She could not *bear* the idea of leaving her home…

But if she didn't, she would lose the Folly for ever. *For ever.* Perspiration beaded her upper lip. Her shoulders dropped in defeat. In the short term, what choice did she have but to play along with Luca's demands? And that meant going to Italy with Zia. Before she could lose her nerve, she dug a couple of suitcases out of a box room further down the corridor. She packed them with a hastily chosen selection of her clothing and her daughter's, squeezing in toys until both cases bulged.

A quiet knock sounded on the bedroom door.

It was Benito. His face a study of careful solemnity, he

passed her several sheets of neatly trimmed fax paper. 'This was on the machine in the library when I went to use it, *signora.*'

Her fair complexion awash with disconcerted pink as she glimpsed the topmost page, which bore a recognisable picture of Luca, she said stiffly, 'You work for Luca?'

'As his executive assistant, *signora.*'

Closing the door again, wondering in hot-cheeked chagrin if Luca had personally censored the information sent by Richard or if, indeed, he considered her efforts to learn about him a source of amusement rather then a worrying development, Darcy spread the results of her former fiancé's surf on the Internet across the bed.

Then she started reading. A piece entitled 'Billion Kill on Wall Street'. It was three months old. Luca was described as a finance magnate, brilliant at playing the world currency markets, born rich and getting even richer. His personal fortune was estimated in a string of noughts that needed counting and incredulous re-counting before she could suspend scepticism. *And this is the guy who took a cheque from me when I was stony broke and he knew it…?* Darcy thought in numbed disbelief.

He was a louse—lower than a louse, even. He was microscopic bacteria! He had no honour, no decency, no shame, no scruples. She read on. Reference was made to Luca's reputation as a commitment-shy womaniser, his ruthless business practices, his implacable nature, his complete lack of sentiment. Darcy was chilled by the perusal of such accolades, and soon decided that it was better not to read any more because it was in all likelihood ninety per cent rubbish and gossip.

No Fielding had ever been guilty of running away from a fight, she reminded herself fiercely. But her problems with the estate were all financial, and Luca had probably been the sort of child who'd started investing his pocket money and playing the stock market at the age of six. She was outmatched, and she felt quite sick at the memory of having confided in him about her overdraft.

Even allowing for exaggeration, Luca was evidently a strikingly effective financial strategist. He was rich, feared and envied, doubtless used to wielding enormous power and influence. A control freak? She glanced down at the grainy picture. So forbidding, so severe, so utterly and completely unlike the male she had fallen madly in love with in Venice. But so dauntingly, chillingly like the male she had married today...

Nothing she had read suggested that he was secretly insane, or given to peculiar starts and fancies, but she was not one bit closer to solving the mystery of his motivation in seeking to punish her. What did he want to punish her *for?* What had she done? She had spent only one night with him, yet for some inexplicable reason he had gone to huge lengths to track her down and hog-tie her by deception into a marriage that had never been intended to be anything but a sham. In achieving that feat, Luca now had the ability to influence and ultimately control her every move over the next six months. The price of defiance would be the loss of everything she held dear.

And although she didn't want to do it, she made herself remember that night in Venice, when her explosive response to his first kiss had shocked her inside out. Within seconds, Darcy was plunging back into the past—indeed, suddenly stung into eagerly seeking out those memories, almost as if some part of her believed they might be a comfort...

'I said just one dance before I leave,' she reminded Luca stiffly, thoroughly unnerved by her own behaviour and pulling hurriedly back from him.

For Richard had never *once* made her feel like that. Only now did she understand why her relationship with the younger man had failed. Neither of them had made an effort to share a bed before their wedding. Richard had said he didn't mind waiting. Theirs had been a love without a spark of passion, an unsentimental fondness which they had both mistaken for something deeper.

'Why should you leave?' Luca demanded.

'I don't belong here—'

He vented a soft, amused laugh. 'Running scared all of a sudden?'

'I'm not scared. I—'

'Are you committed to someone else?'

Recalling Richard's betrayal, fiery pride made her eyes flash. 'I don't believe in commitment!'

'If only that was the truth,' Luca drawled, supremely unimpressed by that declaration. 'In my experience all women ultimately want and expect commitment, no matter what they say in the beginning.'

Darcy flashed him a look of supreme scorn. Having come within inches of the deepest commitment a man could make to a woman and lost out, she no longer had any faith in the worth and security of promises. 'But I don't follow the common herd...haven't you realised that yet?'

As she stepped back from him, he shot out a hand and linked his fingers firmly with hers to keep her close. 'Either you're bitter...or extremely clever.'

'No, frank...and easily bored.'

'Not when I kiss you—'

'You *stopped!*' she condemned.

An appreciative smile of intense amusement slashed his dark features. 'We were attracting attention. I'm not a fan of public displays.'

In the mood to fight with her own shadow, Darcy shrugged. 'Then you're too sedate, too cautious, too conventional for me...'

And, like Neanderthal man reacting with reckless spontaneity to a challenge, Luca hauled her back into his arms and crushed her mouth with fierce, hungry passion under his again. When she had emerged, her lips tingling, every sense leaping with vibrant excitement and delighted pride at this proof of her feminine powers to provoke, she had giggled. 'I liked that…I liked that very much. But I'm still going to leave.'

'You can't—'

'Watch me…' Sashaying her slim but curvaceous hips, she had spun in her low-heeled pumps and moved towards the doors that stood open on the ballroom, willing him to follow her with every fibre of her being.

'If you walk out of here, you will never see me again…'

'Cuts both ways,' she murmured playfully over one slight shoulder, and then she recalled that he was a waiter…or *was* he? Somehow that didn't seem quite as likely as it had earlier.

'*Are* you a waiter?' she paused to ask uncertainly. 'Because if you are, I'm not playing fair.'

'What would you like me to be?'

'Don't be facetious—'

'So that treatment *doesn't* cut both ways! Of course I am not a waiter,' he countered in impatient dismissal.

She smiled then. So he had lifted a tray and brought her a drink specifically to approach *her*. She was impressed, incredibly flattered as well. 'Then you're a guest, a legitimate one, yet you're not masked.'

'I'm—'

'You really are dying to introduce yourself, aren't you? I don't want to know… After tonight, I'll never see you again. What would be the point?'

'You might be surprised—'

'I don't think so…are you going to follow me out of here?'

'*No,*' he delivered with level cool.

'OK…fine. I felt like company, but I'm sure I can find that elsewhere…but then I sort of like you—the way you kiss anyway,' she admitted baldly.

'One moment you behave like a grown woman, the next you talk like a schoolgirl.'

Darcy's face burned with chagrin. As she attempted to

stalk off he tugged her back to him and spoke in a lazy tone of indulgence. 'Tell me, what *would* you like to do tonight that you cannot do here?'

She put her head to one side and answered on impulse. 'Sail in a gondola in the moonlight…'

Luca flinched with almost comical immediacy. 'Not my style. Tourist territory.'

Darcy pulled her fingers free of his. 'I am a tourist. I *dare* you.'

'I'll arrange a trip for you tomorrow—'

'Too late.'

'Then sadly, we are at an impasse.'

'It's your loss.' With a careless jerk of one shapely shoulder, Darcy strolled back into the ballroom. She took her time strolling, but he didn't catch up with her as she had hoped. She wondered why she was playing such dangerous games. She wondered if, her whole life through, she would ever again meet a man who could turn her bones to water and her brain to mush with a single kiss…

On that thought, her stroll slowed to a complete crawl. She glanced back in the direction she had come and froze, suddenly horrified by the discovery that she couldn't pick him out from all the other guests milling about on the edge of the dance floor. Already he was lost.

'Blackmail leaves me cold,' a familiar and undeniably welcome drawl husked in her ear from behind, making her jump a split second before a huge surge of relief washed over her, leaving her weak. 'But that look of pure panic soothes my ego!'

Whirling round, she laughed a little uneasily. 'I wasn't—'

'It is rather frightening to feel like this, isn't it, *cara?*'

'I don't know what you mean—'

'Oh, yes, you do…stay frank, I prefer it.'

'How do you feel about one-night stands?' she asked daringly.

He stilled. A silence thick as fog sprang up.

'I don't do them,' he said drily. 'I was rather hoping you didn't either.'

'How do you feel about virgins?'

'Deeply unexcited.'

'OK, you don't ask me any questions, I won't tell you any lies…how's that for a ground rule?'

'You'll soon get bored with those limitations,' he stated with supreme confidence.

But she *knew* she would not. Honest answers would expose the reality she longed to escape. The young woman who had disappointed from birth by being a girl, who had been denied the opportunity even to continue her education, and who had finally crowned her inadequacies by being jilted at the altar, subjecting her family, to whom appearances were everything, to severe embarrassment and herself to bitter recriminations. She had no desire to pose as an object of pity.

Within minutes he led her down that grand staircase. Realising only then that she had won and that they were leaving the ball together, she stretched up on her toes to kiss him in the crowded hall, generous in victory. Hearing what sounded like a startled buzz of comment erupt around them, she drew back, stunned by her own audacity. She blushed, but he just laughed.

'You're so natural with me,' he breathed appreciatively. 'As if you've known me all your life…'

A magnificent beribboned gondola was moored outside, awaiting their command. A gondola with a cabin swathed in richly embroidered fabric and soft velvet cushions within. And what followed *was* magical. Luca didn't just point out the sights, he entertained her with stories that entranced her. The Palazzo Mocenigo, where Lord Byron had stayed and where one of his many distraught mistresses threw herself from a balcony. The debtor's prison cell from which Casanova contrived a daring escape. The Rialto where Shakespeare's Shylock walked.

His beautiful voice slowly turned husky with hoarseness,

and captured in that haze of romantic imagery she smiled dreamily, sensing his deep love and pride in the city of his birth, reaching up to him to kiss him and meet those dark deep-set eyes with a bubbling assurance she had never experienced in male company before. At one point they glided to a halt in a quiet side canal to be served champagne and strawberries by a sleepy-eyed but smiling waiter.

'You're a fake, *cara mia*,' Luca breathed mockingly then. 'You say you don't want romance, but you revel in every slushy embellishment I can provide.'

'I'm not a fake. Why can't we have *one* perfect night? No strings, no ties, no regrets?'

'I'll make you a bet—a sure-fire certainty,' Luca murmured with silken assurance. 'Whatever happens tonight, I'll meet you tomorrow at three on the Ponte della Guerra. You *will* be there.'

'Tomorrow doesn't exist for us,' she returned dismissively, not even grasping at that point that he might understand her better than she understood herself, that almost the minute she was away from him she would want to be back with him, no matter what the risk. 'Take me home,' she told him then, impatient of the deeply inhibiting need to keep her hands off him in public.

'Where are you staying?'

'*Your* home...'

'We'll have breakfast together—'

'I'm not hungry.'

He had stared steadily down at her. 'You know nothing about me.'

'I know I want to be with you...I know you want to be with me...what *more* do I need to know?'

A spasm of stark pain infiltrated Darcy as she recalled that foolish question. It shot her right back to the present, where fearful uncertainty and frustration ruled. At that moment she could not bear to relive the final hours she had spent with Luca in Venice. And she was tormented by the awareness that her own behaviour that night had been far more reckless, provocative and capricious than she had ever been prepared to admit in the years since.

The door opened without warning. Taken by surprise, Darcy scrambled awkwardly off the bed. Thrusting the door closed again, Luca surveyed her, sensual mouth curling as he scanned the shabby shrunken jeans. 'I always used to believe that a woman without vanity would be an incredible find. Then fate served me with you,' he imparted grimly. 'Now I know better.'

'What's that supposed to mean?' Darcy snapped defensively.

'You'll find out. Sloth in the vanity department won't be a profitable proposition.'

His frowning attention falling on the large framed photo, Luca strode across the room to lift it from the cabinet. There was a stark little silence. He was very still, his chiselled profile clenched taut. 'You sleep with a picture of Richard Carlton by your bed?' he breathed a tinge unevenly, a slightly forced edge to the enquiry that thickened his accent.

'Why not…? We're still very close.' Darcy saw nothing strange in that admission, particularly when her mind was preoccupied with more pressing problems. She drew in a sharp breath. 'Luca…I don't know what's going on here. This whole situation is so crazy, I feel…I feel like Alice in Wonderland after she went through the looking glass!'

'You astonish me. In every depiction I have ever seen Alice sported fabulous long curly hair and a pretty dress. The resemblance is in *your* mind alone.'

Darcy groaned. 'Now you're being flippant. From my point of view you are acting like a man who has escaped from an asylum—'

'That is because you have an extremely prosaic outlook,' Luca delivered softly. 'You cannot grasp the concept of revenge because you yourself would consider revenge a waste of time and effort. I too am practical, but I warn you,

I also have great imagination and a constitutional inability to live with being bested by anyone. Setting the police on your trail wouldn't have given me the slightest satisfaction—'

'The...the *police?*' Darcy stressed with a look of blank astonishment.

Luca flicked her a shrewd, narrow-eyed glance, eyes black and cold as a wintry night. 'You play the innocent so well. I can ever understand why. You were far from home. You felt secure in the belief that you would never be identified, never be traced, never be punished for your dishonesty—'

'I don't know what the blazes you're talking about!' Darcy spluttered. 'My...*dishonesty?*'

'But you miscalculated...the role of victim is not for me,' Luca declared. 'And now it's your turn to savour the same experience. A flare for the prosaic will be of no benefit whatsoever in the weeks to come.'

'I've got a lot more staying power than you think!' Darcy fired back, determined to stand up to him. 'So why don't you tell me why you're making crazy references to the police and my supposed dishonesty?'

Luca sent her a winging glance of derision. 'Why waste my breath? I prefer to wait until you get tired of pretending and decide to make a pathetic little confession about how temptation got the better of you!'

'I can hardly confess to something I haven't done!' Darcy objected in vehement frustration.

Ignoring that fierce protest, Luca lifted up a sheet of the fax paper, directing his attention to the business address of the stud farm at the top. 'Carlton's place,' he registered grimly. 'So it was Carlton you got in touch with.'

'I didn't tell Richard anything...I just wanted to know who you really were—*not* an unreasonable wish when I find myself married to a man who hasn't told me one single word of truth!' Darcy shot at him in ringing condemnation.

'But you couldn't wait to get married to me,' Luca reminded her with gentle irony. 'And, I, who have never felt the tiniest urge to give up my freedom, was equally eager in this instance to see the legal bond put in place.'

'Because now you think you've got me where you want me.'

Luca regarded her with hard intensity. His arrogant dark head tipped back. Eyes hard as diamonds raked her defiant face. 'Carlton's still your lover, isn't he?'

'That's none of your business…in fact if I had a lover for every different day of the week, it would be none of your business!' Darcy slung back.

'No?' Luca said softly.

'No!' As her temper rode higher, Darcy was indifferent to the menace of that velvet-soft intonation.

Luca shifted a lean dark hand with fluid grace and eloquence. 'Even the suspicion that you could be contemplating infidelity will be grounds for separation. You see, although I have laid it all before you in very simple terms, you still fail to appreciate that I hold every card. You cannot afford to antagonise a husband you need to retain.'

Darcy shivered with anger, outraged by that, 'very simple terms', which suggested she was of less than average intelligence. 'The price could well be too high—'

'But it *has* to be high, and more than you want to pay…how could I enjoy this otherwise?' Luca countered, the dark planes of his strikingly handsome features bearing a look of calm enquiry.

As her green eyes flashed with sheer fury, Luca shot her a provocative smile.

In that instant, Darcy lost her head. Temper blazing, she stalked forward and lifted a hand with which to slap that hateful smile into eternity. With a throaty sound of infuriating amusement, Luca sidestepped her. Closing two strong hands round her narrow ribcage, he lifted her clean off her feet and tumbled her down onto the bed behind her.

# CHAPTER SIX

BREATHLESS and stunned as Luca captured her furiously flailing hands in one of his, Darcy whispered in outrage, 'What do you think you're doing?'

'I'm not thinking right now,' Luca confided, luxuriant lashes low on liquid golden eyes of sensual appraisal as he scanned the riot of bright curls on her small head. 'I'm wondering how long your hair will get in six months... You'll grow it for me, just as you will do so many other things *just* for me—'

'*Dream on!*'

Confident eyes gleamed down into scorching green.

As Luca slowly lowered his lean, well-built body down onto hers, a jolt of sexual awareness as keen and sharp as an electric shock currented through Darcy. The sensation made her even more determined to break free.

Luca banded both arms more fully round her violently struggling figure. 'Calm down...you'll hurt yourself!' he urged impatiently.

'You are in the wrong position to tell me to do that!' Darcy warned breathlessly.

'Assault would be grounds for separation too,' Luca informed her indolently.

Darcy's knee tingled. She, who had never in her entire life hurt another human being, now longed to deliver a crippling blow. Luca contemplated her with almost scientific interest, making no attempt to protect himself. 'I want to hurt you!' she suddenly screeched at him in driven fury.

'But this crumbling pile of bricks and mortar stands between you and that desire,' Luca guessed with galling accuracy. 'It will be interesting to see how much you will tolerate before you snap and surrender.'

Darcy's blood ran cold at that unfeeling response.

'You'll play the whore in my bed for the sake of this house...but then what you've already done once should come even more easily a second time,' Luca surmised icily.

'You're talking rubbish, because I'll never sleep with you...I will *never* sleep with you again!' In a wild movement of repudiation, Darcy garnered the strength to tear herself free. But Luca had frighteningly fast reflexes. With a rueful sigh over her obstinacy, he snapped long fingers round her shoulder before she could move out of reach, and simply tipped her back into his arms.

'Of course you will,' he countered levelly then, brilliant dark eyes locked to her furiously flushed face.

'I *won't!*' Darcy swore.

As Luca slowly anchored her back to the mattress with his superior body weight, the all pervasive heat of his big, powerful frame engulfed her limbs in a drugging paralysis. Momentarily Darcy forgot to struggle. She also forgot to breathe.

Luca angled down his arrogant dark head and tasted her soft mouth with a devastatingly direct hunger that shot right down to her toes. Her lips burned; her thighs trembled. She looked up at him in complete shock, her mind wiped clean of thought. But her heart pounded as if she was fighting for her life, her pupils dilated, her breath coming in tiny frantic pants. She collided with the blaze of sexual challenge in his gaze and it was as if he had thrown the switch on her self-control. Dear heaven, she loved it when he looked at her like *that*...

Deep down inside, she melted with terrifying anticipation of the excitement to come. Her breasts stirred inside her cotton bra, nipples peaking with painful suddenness into taut, straining buds. Luca shifted and she felt the hard, masculine thrust of his erection against her pelvis. She quivered, her spine arching as her yielding body flooded with liquid heat and surrender. Neither one of them heard the soft rap on the bedroom door.

His dark eyes burned gold with fierce satisfaction. He rimmed her parted lips with the tip of his tongue, teasing, taunting, the warmth of his breath fanning her, locking her into breathless intimacy. Every atom of her being was desperate for his next move, the moist, sensitive interior of her mouth aching for his penetration.

'Fight me...' Luca instructed huskily. 'After all the fun of the chase, an easy victory would be a real disappointment.'

Almost simultaneously, a loud knock thudded on the sturdy door. Darcy flinched and jerked up her knee in fright, accidentally connecting with Luca's anatomy in an unfortunate place. As he wrenched back from her in stunned pain and incredulity Darcy cried, 'Oh, no...*gosh*, I'm sorry!' and she reeled off the bed like a drunk, frantically smoothing down her rumpled sweater and striving to walk in a straight line to the door.

'Is Luca with you, *signora?*' Benito enquired levelly. 'The helicopter has arrived early.'

Hearing a muffled groan from somewhere behind her, Darcy coughed noisily to conceal the sound, and with crimson cheeks she muttered defensively, 'I don't know where he is...and we can't leave yet anyway. I have hens to feed.'

'Hens...' Benito echoed, and nodded very slowly at that information.

Closing the door again, and tactfully not looking in Luca's direction, Darcy whispered in considerable embarrassment, 'Are you all right, Luca?'

Luca gritted something that didn't sound terribly reassuring in his own language.

'I'll get you a glass of water,' Darcy proffered, full of genuine remorse. 'It was an accident...honestly, it was—'

'Bitch...' Luca ground out with agonised effort.

Darcy withdrew a step. The silence thundered.

'I'll see you later,' she muttered curtly. 'Right now, I've got work to do.'

'We're flying to Venice!' Luca shot at her rawly.

Only then did Darcy also recall the appointment she had made at the bank. Checking her watch, she emitted a strangled groan and took flight.

Half an hour later, having mucked out Nero's stable, Darcy mustered the courage to enter the poultry coop. Henrietta the hen, who regarded every human invasion as a hostile act, gave her a mean look of anticipation.

'Please, Henrietta, *not* today,' Darcy pleaded as she hurriedly filled a bowl with eggs, her thoughts straying helplessly back to Luca and the excruciating awareness that he could still rip away her defences and make her agonisingly vulnerable.

She was so desperately confused by the emotions flailing her. She knew now that prior to the revelation of Luca's real identity she had grown to trust him, *like* him, even. She had revelled in his sophisticated cool at Margo's party, his seeming protectiveness, even the envious looks of other women. Dear God, how pathetic she had been, and now she felt gutted, absolutely gutted by the most savage sense of loss and bewilderment, and quite incapable of comprehending what was going on inside her own head.

And as for her wretched body...? Recalling that kiss on the bed, reliving the shameless and eager anticipation which had flamed through her, Darcy hated herself. Luca had been taunting her, humiliating her with her own weakness. The tables had been turned with a vengeance, she acknowledged painfully. For hadn't she foolishly believed for the space of one night three years ago that she, too, could treat sex as a casual experience for which pleasure would be the only price?

Hadn't she been bitterly conscious that night in Venice that she was still a virgin? Hadn't she been rebelling against her own image? Hadn't she longed to taste the power of being a sexually aware and sexually appealing woman?

And hadn't the idea of throwing off her inhibitions far from home been tempting? And hadn't she known the same moment Luca melted her bones with one passionate kiss that she wanted to go to bed with him and forever banish the demeaning memory of her sterile, sexless relationship with Richard?

And, worse, hadn't she thrown herself at Luca at every opportunity, stubbornly evading his every attempt to slow the pace of their intimacy? All that champagne on top of her medication had left her bereft of every inhibition. For so long she had used the alcohol in her veins as an excuse. But the imagery that now assailed Darcy in split-second shattering Technicolor frames, the undeniably shocking memories of how she had treated Luca that night, now filled her with choking shame.

She had never once allowed herself to remember exactly what she had done to Luca in that bedroom. She had been in the grip of a wanton hunger, a hunger fanned to white-hot heat by the knowledge that this beautiful, gorgeous, sophisticated guy was weak with lust for *her*. She hadn't wanted him to suspect that he was her first lover...and she had gone to indecent lengths not to give him the smallest grounds for that suspicion.

As a pained moan of mortification escaped Darcy under the assault of those memories, Henrietta jabbed a vicious beak into her extended hand.

With a startled yelp of pain, Darcy exited backwards from the coop, her dogs barking frantically at her heels.

'*Sta zitto!*' That command slashed through the air like a whip.

Darcy twisted round in dismay. In the light of her recent thoughts she was truly appalled to see Luca poised on the path several feet away. Her face flamed. There he was, six feet four inches of staggeringly attractive, sleek and powerful masculinity, luxuriant black hair smooth, charcoal-grey suit shrieking class and expensive tailoring. But, disconcertingly, Darcy's defiant subconscious threw up a much more disturbing image of Luca. Luca sprawled gloriously naked across white sheets, a magnificent vision of golden-skinned male perfection, a life-sized fantasy toy entirely at her mercy.

Far, far too late had she learnt that Luca had inspired her with something infinitely more dangerous than desire. He would laugh longest and loudest if he ever realised that truth.

Suddenly sick with pain and regret at her own stupidity, Darcy twisted her bright head away under the onslaught of those fiercely intelligent dark eyes.

As Humpf and Bert grovelled ingratiatingly round his feet, Luca scanned Darcy's bedraggled appearance. Her jeans were streaked with dirt, her sweater liberally adorned with pieces of straw. Dawning disbelief in his grim appraisal, he breathed with admirable restraint, 'You have exactly ten minutes to change and board the helicopter.'

'I can't!' Darcy protested, her evasive eyes whipping back in his general direction. 'I have to go to the bank—'

'Why? Are you planning to rob it?' Luca enquired sardonically. 'If I was your bank manager, nothing short of an armed assault would persuade me to advance you any further credit!'

Darcy compressed her lips in a mutinous line.

'No bank,' said Luca. 'We have a take-off slot to make at the airport.'

'I *can't* miss this appointment—'

Luca caught her by the elbow as she attempted to stalk past him. 'You're bleeding…what have you done to yourself?' he demanded.

Darcy flicked an irritable glance down at the angry scratch oozing blood on the back of her hand. 'It's nothing. Henrietta's always attacking me.'

'Henrietta?'

'Queen of the coop—the hen with attitude. I ought to wring her manic neck, but she'd come back and haunt me.

In a strange way, I'm sort of fond of her,' Darcy admitted grudgingly. 'She's got personality.'

Luca's intent dark eyes now held a slightly dazed aspect. He was no Einstein on the subject of hens, she registered.

Darcy took advantage of his abstraction to pull free. 'I'll be back before you know it…I promise!' she slung over her shoulder as she sped off.

It took her ten minutes to change into the tweed skirt and tailored blouse she always wore to the bank. Studiously ignoring the helicopter sitting on the front lawn, and the pilot pacing up and down beside it, she jumped into the Land Rover and rattled off down the drive.

Two hours later, having been to the bank, and then arranged for a local farmer to pick up and stable Nero, Darcy walked into Karen's kitchen to ask her to look after the dogs, feed the hens from a safe distance and keep an eye on the Folly.

Zia bounced up into her mother's arms. Darcy studied her daughter's clear dark eyes, smooth golden skin and ebony curls. A sinking sensation curdled her stomach. From her classic little nose to her feathery but dead level brows, Zia looked so *like* her father. Darcy buried her face in her daughter's springy hair and breathed in the fresh, clean scent of her child while she fought to master emotions and fears that were dangerously near to the surface. In fact, all she wanted to do at that instant was collapse into floods of overwrought tears, and the knowledge appalled her.

'Benito's been down twice to see if you're here…talk about fussing!' Karen told her above the toddler's animated chatter. 'What's all this about you going to Italy?'

'Don't ask,' Darcy advised flatly. 'I've just been to the bank. My bank manager says he's not a betting man.'

'I could've told you that without seeing him. He's so miserable, he wouldn't bet on the sun rising tomorrow!'

'He said that in six months' time, when I actually inherit, it'll be different, but that it would be wrong to allow me to borrow more now on the strength of what are only ex-

pectations.' That Luca had made the same forecast right off
the top of his superior head infuriated Darcy.

'I'm really sorry…' Karen's eyes, however, remained
bright with curiosity. 'But if you've got five minutes could
you possibly tell me where the swanky limo and the helicopter have come from?'

'They belong to Luca.'

'So he *was* a dark horse. How very strange! People usually pretend to be more than they are rather than *less* than
they are. Was Nina right, after all? Has he married you to
gain a British passport?' Karen pressed with a frown. 'Why
all the heavy secrecy? He's not one of these high-flying
international criminals, is he?'

If Luca *had* been a criminal, the police might just have
been able to take him away, Darcy thought helplessly. But
then that wouldn't have suited her either. No matter how
obnoxious he was, she needed to hang onto her husband
for the next six months. What shook her even more at that
moment was the sudden shattering awareness that in spite
of the manner in which Luca was behaving, the threat of
him disappearing altogether made her feel positively sick
and shaky.

'Darcy…?' Karen prompted.

She averted her attention from her friend. 'There was a
confidentiality clause in our pre-nuptial contract. I'd like to
tell you everything,' she lied, because there was no way
she wanted to tell a living soul about how stupid she had
been, 'but I can't… Will you look after the Folly while I'm
away?'

'Of course I will. I'll move in. Don't look so glum,
Darcy…six months won't be that long in going by.'

But the Folly might well be repossessed long before that
six months was up. Karen's purchase of the gate lodge had
bought some time, by paying off the most pressing debts
against the estate, but Darcy was still a couple of months
behind with the mortgage repayments.

She drove back up to the house and clambered out. Luca

emerged from the entrance, strong, dark face rigid, dark eyes diamond-hard with exasperation.

'Have you any idea what time it is?' he launched at her.

Zia skipped forward. She was unconcerned by that greeting. She had grown up with a grandfather who bawled the length of the room at everybody, and volume bothered her not at all. She extended a foot with a carefully pointed toe for Luca's inspection. 'See…pretty,' she told Luca chirpily.

'*Accidenti*…' Luca began, reluctantly tearing his attention from Darcy to focus with a frown on the tiny child in front of him.

'If you want peace, admire her frilly socks.'

'I beg your pardon?' Luca breathed grittily.

'Zia…' Darcy urged, holding out her hand.

But her daughter was stubborn. Her bottom lip jutted out. She wasn't used to being ignored. In fact, Darcy reflected, if Zia had a fault, it was a pronounced *dislike* of being ignored.

'Has you dot pretty socks?' Zia demanded somewhat aggressively of Luca.

'No, I haven't!' Luca ground out in fierce exasperation.

There was no mistaking that tone of rejection. Zia's eyes grew huge and then flooded with tears. A noisy sob burst from her instantaneously.

Darcy swept up her daughter to comfort her. 'You really are a cruel swine,' she condemned feverishly. 'She's only a baby…and if you think I'm travelling to Italy with someone who treats my child like that, you're insane!'

Discovering that even the loyal Benito, who had come to an uneasy halt some feet away, was regarding him in shocked surprise, Luca felt his blunt cheekbones drench with dark colour. He strode back into the house in Darcy's furious wake.

'I'm sorry…I'm not used to young children,' he admitted stiltedly.

'That's no excuse—'

*'Bad man!'* Zia sobbed accusingly from the security of her mother's arms.

'Never mind, darling.' Darcy smoothed her daughter's tumbled curls.

'You could *try* contradicting her—'

'She'd know I was lying.'

But, mollified by the apology and the certain awareness that Luca had just enjoyed an uncomfortable learning experience, Darcy went back outside and climbed into the helicopter.

'Is she asleep?' Luca skimmed a deeply cautious glance into the sleeping compartment of his private jet to survey the slight immobile bump on the built-in divan, his voice a positive whisper in which prayer and hope were blatant and unashamed.

Darcy tiptoed out into the main cabin, her face grey with fatigue. In all her life she had never endured a more nightmare journey.

Zia had been sick all the way to London in the helicopter. The long wait in the VIP lounge until the jet could get another take-off slot had done nothing to improve the spirits of a distressed, over-tired and still nauseous little girl. Zia had whinged, cried, thrown hysterical tantrums on the carpet beneath Luca's utterly stricken and appalled gaze, and generally conducted herself like the toddler from hell.

'She's never behaved like that before,' Darcy muttered wearily for about the twentieth time.

By now impervious to such statements, Luca sank down with a shell-shocked aspect into a comfortable seat. Then he sat forward abruptly, an aghast set to his lean, dark features. 'Will she wake up again when we land?'

'Heaven knows…' Darcy was afraid to make any more optimistic forecasts, but maternal protectiveness prompted her to speak up in further defence of her daughter. 'Zia's not used to being sick. She likes a secure routine, her own familiar things around her,' she explained. 'Everything's been strange to her, and then when she was hungry and we could only offer her foreign food—'

'That was definitely the last straw,' Luca recalled with a shudder. 'I can still hear those screams. *Per meraviglia…* what a temper she has! And so stubborn, so demanding! I had no idea that one small child could be that disruptive. As for the embarrassment she caused me—'

'All right…*all right!*' Darcy groaned in interruption as she collapsed down into the seat opposite.

'Let me tell you, it is no trivial matter to have to trail a child screaming that I am a *bad man* through a crowded airport!' Luca slammed back at her in wrathful recollection. 'And whose fault was that? Who allowed that phrase to implant in the poor child's head? What I have suffered this evening would have taxed the compassion of a saint!'

Darcy closed her aching eyes. A policeman, clearly alerted by a concerned member of the public, had intervened to request that Luca identify himself. Then a man with a camera and a nasty raucous laugh had taken a photo of them.

The flash of the powerful camera had scared Zia. Darcy had been shaken, it not having previously occurred to her that Luca might be a target for such intrusive press attention. Bereft even of the slight protection that might have been offered by Benito, who had left the Folly in the limousine, Luca had seethed in controlled silence. A saint he was not, but he *had* made a sustained effort to assist her in comforting and calming Zia.

Luca released his breath in a stark hiss. 'However, the original fault was of my own making. When I demanded an immediate departure from your home, I took no account of the needs of so young a child. It was too late in the day to embark on such a journey.'

Kicking off her shoes, Darcy curled her legs wearily beneath her. Such a concession was of little comfort to her now. She was wrung out.

'But this *is* our wedding night,' Luca reminded her, as if that was some kind of excuse.

Darcy didn't even have enough energy left to expel a grizzly laugh at that announcement. She sagged into the luxurious comfort of the seat and rested her head back to survey him with shadowed green eyes.

The sight of Zia asleep and the sound of silence appeared to have revived Luca. His dark eyes glittered with restive energy. He looked neither tired nor under strain, but he was no longer quite so immaculate, she noted, desperate to find comfort in that minor show of human fallibility. He now had a definable five o'clock shadow on his hard jawline. He had also loosened his tie and undone the top button of his shirt to reveal the strong brown column of his throat. And, if anything, he looked even more devastatingly attractive than he had looked at the altar, she acknowledged, and instantly despised herself for noticing.

With great effort, Darcy mustered her thoughts and breathed in deep. 'I have the right to know *why* you're doing this to me, Luca,' she told him yet again.

'But what have I done?' An ebony brow elevated. 'I agreed to marry you and have I not done so?'

Darcy groaned in unconcealed despair. 'Luca…*please!* I hate games. If I'd had the time and the peace at the Folly…if I hadn't been in so much shock at your threats…I wouldn't have allowed you to browbeat and panic me into this trip at such short notice.'

'I planned it that way,' Luca admitted, with the kind of immovable calm that made her want to tear him to pieces.

As her temper flared, colour burnished her cheeks and her eyes sparked with the fire of her frustration. 'You still have to tell me *why* you're doing this to me!' Darcy reminded him with fierce emphasis. 'And if you don't, I will—'

'Yes…what *will* you do?' Luca interposed deflatingly. 'Fly back to the UK alone and accept the loss of that house on which you place such value?'

It was the same threat which had intimidated Darcy into acquiescence that afternoon. But she was now beyond being silenced. 'You insinuated that I had done something dishonest that night in Venice...and that is an outrageous untruth.'

'Theft is a crime. It is never acceptable. But when theft is linked to deliberate deception, it is doubly abhorrent and offensive.' Luca delivered that condemnation with unblemished gravity.

Darcy's temples were beginning to pound with tension again. Her strained eyes locked to his cold, dark gaze. 'Let me get this s-straight,' she whispered, her voice catching in her throat. '*You* are actually accusing *me* of having stolen something from you that night?'

'My overnight guests don't as a rule use a small rear window as an exit,' Luca responded very drily. 'I was downstairs within minutes of the alarm going off!'

Darcy's face flamed with chagrin at the reminder of the manner in which she had been forced to leave his apartment. She had crept out of his bed while he was still asleep. When that horrible shrieking alarm had sounded as she'd climbed out of the window, she had panicked. Dying a thousand deaths in her embarrassment, she had raced down the narrow alley beyond at supersonic speed. 'For heaven's sake, I just wanted to leave quietly...but I couldn't get your blasted front door open!'

'Not without the security code,' Luca conceded. 'It would only have opened without the code if there had been a fire or if I had shut down the system. I was surprised that a thief ingenious enough to beat every other security device in that apartment *and* break into my safe should make such a very clumsy departure.'

'Break into your safe,' Darcy repeated, wide-eyed, weakened further by the revelation that this insane man she had married believed she was not only guilty of having stolen from him but also equal to the challenge of cracking open a safe.

'As a morning-after-the-night-before experience, it was unparalleled,' Luca informed her sardonically.

'I've never stolen anything in my life...I *wouldn't!*' It was a strangled plea of innocence, powered by strong distaste. 'As for breaking into a safe, I wouldn't even know where to *begin!*' Darcy emphasised, eyes dark with disbelief that he could credit otherwise.

Luca searched her shaken face with shrewd intensity and slowly moved his arrogant dark head in reluctant admiration. 'You're even more convincing than I expected you to be.'

In an abrupt movement, Darcy uncoiled her legs and sprang upright to stare down at him. 'You've got to believe me...for heaven's sake...if someone broke into that apartment and stole from you as that day was dawning, it certainly wasn't me!'

'No, I made the very great misjudgement of taking the thief home with me so that she could do an easier inside job,' Luca commented with icy exactitude, his strong jaw clenching. 'And in a sense you're right; it wasn't you. You wore a disguise—'

'Disguise?' Darcy broke in weakly.

'You made the effort to look like a million dollars that night. You had to look the part.'

'Luca—'

'You gatecrashed an élite social function attended by some very wealthy people and were careful not to draw too much attention to yourself,' Luca continued grimly, his expressive mouth hard as iron. 'You refused to identify yourself in any way and you ensured that I brought you home with me...after all, with the number of staff around your chances of contriving to steal anything from the Palazzo d'Oro were extremely slim.'

'I didn't do it...do you hear me?' Darcy almost shrieked at him. '*I didn't do it!*'

Luca dealt her a withering glance of savage amusement.

'But you've already confessed that you did steal *and* sell the ring. Or had you forgotten that reality?'

Darcy's lashes fluttered in bewilderment. Left bereft of breath by that staggering assurance, she pressed a weak hand to her damp brow and tottered backwards into her seat again.

# CHAPTER SEVEN

'DON'T you recall that sleepy and foolish little confession at the inn?' Luca prompted with a scathing look of derision. 'You admitted that the sale of an antique ring financed roof repairs for your family home and indeed may well have staved off the enforced sale of that home.'

'It was a *ring* which was stolen from your safe?' Darcy breathed shakily, belatedly making that connection. 'But that's just a stupid coincidence. The ring that my father sold belonged to my family!'

'The Adorata ring is stolen and only a few months later the Fieldings contrive to rescue their dwindling fortunes by the judicious discovery and sale of *another* ring?' Luca jibed, unimpressed by her explanation. 'There *was* no other ring! And, since your family estate is still in financial hot water, you must've sold the Adorata for a tithe of its true worth!'

'I've never heard of this Ador-whatever ring that you're talking about, nor have I been involved in any way in either stealing or selling it!' Darcy's taut voice shook, her growing exhaustion biting deep.

'You were wise enough to wait a while before selling it and you ensured that it was a private sale. Now I hope you also have sufficient wit to know when your back is up against a brick wall,' Luca spelt out icily. 'I want the name of the buyer. And you had better hope and pray for your own sake that I am able to reclaim the Adorata without resorting to legal intervention!'

'It wasn't your wretched ring. I swear it wasn't!' Darcy protested sharply, appalled by his refusal even to stop and take proper account of her arguments in her own defence.

'I don't know who bought it because my father insisted on dealing with the sale. He was a very proud man. He didn't want *anybody* to know that he was so short of money that he had to sell an heirloom—'

'Why waste my time with these stupid stories?' Luca subjected her to a hard scrutiny, his contempt and his impatience with her protests palpable. 'I despise liars. Before I put you back out of my life, you will tell me where that ring is...or you will lose by it.'

It occurred to Darcy then that no matter what she did with Luca, he intended her to lose by it. He had hemmed her in with so many threats she felt trapped. And the shattering revelation that he believed her to be a thief equal to safe-cracking just seemed to stop her weary brain functioning altogether.

Only two thoughts stayed in her mind. Luca might still be walking around as if he was sane, but he couldn't be. And possibly he had been watching too many movies in which incredibly immoral calculating women seduced the hero and then turned on him with evil intent. Safe-cracking? A glazed look in her eyes, Darcy contemplated the fact that she couldn't even operate a washing machine without going step by painful step through the instructions...

'Do you still find it magical?' Luca demanded, above the roar of the motorboat which had collected them from Marco Polo Airport to waft them across the lagoon into the city.

A woman in a waking dream, Darcy gazed out on the Grand Canal. The darkness was dispelled by the lights in the beautiful medieval buildings and on the other craft around them. The grand, sweeping waterway throbbed with life. It was like travelling inside a magnificent painting, she thought privately. She assumed that they were heading to his apartment, but as far as she was concerned they could happily spend the rest of the night getting there.

When the boatman chugged into a mooring at the

Palazzo d'Oro, with its splendid Renaissance façade, Darcy was astonished. 'Why are we stopping here?'

'This is my home,' Luca informed her.

'But it c-can't be…' Darcy stammered.

Deftly detaching Zia's solid little body from her arms, Luca stepped out onto the covered walkway semi-screened from the canal by an elaborate run of pillars and arches. At the entrance to the *palazzo,* an older woman in an apron stood in readiness. She made clucking sounds and extended sturdy arms to receive the sleeping child.

Darcy snatched at Luca's hand and stepped out onto the walkway. 'Who's that?'

'My sister Ilaria's old nursemaid. She will put Zia to bed and stay with her.'

'But I—'

As Luca urged her into the spectacular entrance hall, with its glorious domed ceiling frescoes far above, Darcy stilled. 'You *can't* live here—'

'My ancestors *built* the Palazzo d'Oro.'

Just as Luca finished speaking, a startling interruption occurred. Two enormous shaggy dogs loped noisily down the fantastic gilded staircase pursued by a shouting middle-aged manservant.

*'Santo cielo!'* Luca rapped out a sharp command that forestalled the threatening surge of boisterous animal greeting. The deerhounds fell back, tails drooping between their impossibly long legs, great narrow heads lowered, doggy brown eyes pathetic in their disappointment.

The manservant broke into a flood of anxious explanation. Luca turned back to Darcy, exasperation etched in his lean, strong features.

'What are they called?' Darcy prompted eagerly.

'Aristide and Zou Zou,' Luca divulged reluctantly, his nostrils flaring. 'They belong to my sister.'

'Aren't they gorgeous?' Darcy began to move forward to pet the two dogs.

As a pair of very long tails began to rise in response to

that soft, encouraging intonation, Luca closed an arm round his bride to restrain her enthusiasm. 'No, they are *not*,' he stressed meaningfully. 'They are undisciplined, unbelievably stupid and wholly unsuited to city life. But every time Ilaria goes away, she dumps them here.'

As Luca's manservant gripped their jewel-studded collars to lead them away, the two dogs twisted their heads back to focus on Darcy with pleading eyes. She was touched to the heart.

'Are you hungry?' Luca asked then.

'I couldn't eat to save my life.'

'Then I will show you upstairs.'

'If this is really your home,' Darcy whispered numbly about halfway up the second flight. 'That means...that means that you were the *host* at the masked ball.'

'You wouldn't let me tell you who I was. And since the ball invariably lasts until dawn, I could scarcely bring you back here for the remainder of the night. At the time, I had been using the apartment regularly while renovations were being carried out here.'

'There's so much I don't know about you—'

'And now you have all the time in the world to discover everything you ever wanted to know,' Luca pointed out in a tone of bracing consolation.

'I don't think I want to find out any more.'

'This has not been the most propitious of wedding days,' Luca conceded smoothly. 'But I'm certain you have the resilience to rise above a somewhat difficult beginning. After all, *cara mia*...I'm prepared to be very generous.'

Darcy gawped at him. *'Generous?'*

'If you satisfy my demands, I *will* allow you to inherit that one million. I'm not a complete bastard. There are those who say that I am,' Luca admitted reflectively, 'and I would concede that I am no bleeding heart, but I am always scrupulously fair in my dealings.'

'Is that a fact?' Darcy passed no opinion because she didn't have the energy to argue with him.

Passing down a corridor lined with fine oil paintings, Luca flung open the door of a superb bedroom full of ornate gilded furniture. One stunned glance was sufficient to tell Darcy that in comparison Fielding's Folly offered all the comfort of a medieval barn in an advanced state of decay.

'Your luggage will be brought up.'

'I want to see Zia. Where is she?'

'In the nursery suite on the floor above. Most mothers would be grateful for a break from childcare on their wedding night.'

'What is with this "wedding night" bit you keep on mentioning?' Darcy enquired with stilted reluctance.

Luca treated her to a slow, sensual smile. Dark golden eyes of intent gleamed below luxuriant black lashes. 'You are not that naive. Whatever else you may be, you are still a Raffacani bride, and tonight in the time-honoured tradition of my ancestors we will share that bed together.'

Darcy thought about this nightmare day she had enjoyed at Luca's merciless hands. She studied him in honest disbelief.

'You should congratulate yourself.' His exquisitely expressive mouth quirked. 'Only the memory of that incredibly passionate night we once shared persuaded me to go to the extremity of marrying you. The prospect of six sexually self-indulgent months played a major part in that decision.'

'I can imagine,' Darcy mumbled weakly, and she *could*.

Luca saw life's every event in terms of profit and loss. Almost three years ago he had suffered a loss for which he had falsely blamed her. Now he planned to turn loss into vengeful profit between the bedsheets. It was novel, she conceded. But for a rogue male to whom everything probably came far too easily, anything that supplied a challenge would always be what he wanted most.

Dear heaven, had she been that exciting in bed? She had been imaginative, she was prepared to admit, but that night had been a one-off. Heady romance, bitter rebellion and

fiery desire had combined with champagne to send her off
the rails. She had lived out a never to be repeated kind of
fantasy and lived on to regret every single second of her
reckless misbehaviour.

'I'll give you an hour to rediscover your energies and
ponder the reality that a marriage that is *not* consummated
is worthless in the eyes of the law.'

'What are you talking about?'

'Aren't you aware that sex is an integral part of the marriage contract? And the lack of it grounds for annulment?'

Darcy's jaw dropped.

'You see, I'm not a complete bastard,' Luca contended,
smooth as glass. 'A complete bastard would have left you
to sleep in ignorance and gone for non-consummation at
the end of the six months.'

Leaving her to reflect on that revelation of astounding
generosity, Luca strolled back out of the room.

That is one happy man, Darcy thought helplessly. An
utterly ruthless male with the persistence of a juggernaut,
punch-drunk on the belief that he had her exactly where he
wanted her. He was destined to discover that he had a pro-
longed battle ahead of him. Although she was currently at
a very low ebb, Darcy was by nature a fighter.

A thief. He thought she was a thief. He genuinely believed that she had stolen that wretched ring with the stupid
name. And, truth to tell, if it had been stolen the same night,
he had some grounds for that suspicion. Indeed, when that
theft was combined with her flight at dawn, her status as a
gatecrasher and her flat refusal to tell him who she was
throughout the evening, she had to concede that his conviction that she was the guilty party *was* based on some
pretty solid-looking facts.

However, those facts were simply misleading facts.
Obviously she had been in the wrong place at the wrong
time. But Luca wasn't the type of male likely to question
his own judgement. In fact, unless she was very much mistaken, Luca prided himself on his powers of logic and rea-

soning. That being so, for almost three years he had staunchly believed that she was the culprit. By now, the real thief and the ring had to be long gone. Luca's mistake, not hers.

In the meantime, only by finding some proof that the ring her father had sold had been a different ring entirely could she hope to defend herself. Had her father kept any record of that sale? And what the heck was the use of wondering that when she was stuck in Venice and unable to conduct any sort of search? Why, oh, why had she allowed Luca to steamroller her into flying straight to Italy?

And the answer came back loud and clear. If she had refused, Luca would have gone without her. Challenged at the very outset of their marriage, Luca would have carried through on that threat.

An hour later, Luca sauntered back into the marital bedroom and stopped dead only halfway towards the canopied bed.

Contented canine snores alerted him to the presence of at least one four-legged intruder. And there was no room for a bridegroom in the bed, vast as it was. Darcy lay dead centre, one arm curved protectively round her slumbering daughter, the other draped across two enormous shaggy backs.

Zou Zou was snoring like a train. Aristide opened his eyes, and in his efforts to conceal himself did a comic impression of a very large dog trying to shrink himself to the size of a chihuahua. Pushing his head bashfully between his paws, perfectly aware that he was not allowed on the bed, he surveyed Luca pleadingly, unaware that the child on the other side of the bed was his most powerful source of protection.

Luca drew in a slow, steadying breath and backed towards the door very quietly. He had learnt considerable respect for the consequences of *not* letting sleeping toddlers lie…

\* \* \*

Darcy was nudged awake at half past six in the morning by the dogs.

After a brisk wash in her usual cold water in the *en suite* bathroom, she trudged downstairs in her checked pyjamas and old wool dressing gown, startling the dapper little man-servant breakfasting in the sleek, ultra-modern kitchen on the ground floor. Beneath the older man's aghast gaze, she fed and watered the dogs and refused to allow him to interrupt his meal. She then insisted on charring two croissants and brewing some not very successful coffee for herself. She wrinkled her nose as she ate and drank. Cooking had never been her metier, but her digestion was robust.

Finding Zia still soundly asleep when she returned to the bedroom, she succumbed to the notion of returning to bed to give her daughter a cuddle, but while in the act of waiting for the toddler to awaken naturally she contrived to drift off to sleep again.

The second time she woke up, she stretched luxuriantly. Then, as she recalled rising earlier, she was seized by instant guilt and wondered with all the horror of someone who never, ever had a lie-in what time it was.

'It's a quarter past nine, *cara mia*,' a deep, dark drawl responded to the anxious question she had unwittingly said out loud.

That reply so alarmingly close to hand acted like a cattle prod on Darcy. Eyes flying wide in dismay, she flipped over to her side to confront her uninvited companion. 'Good heavens...a q-quarter past nine?' she stuttered. 'Where's Zia?'

'Breakfasting upstairs in the nursery suite.'

His clean-shaven jaw supported by an indolent hand, Luca gazed down at Darcy's startled face with a slow, mocking smile that made her pulses race. Her shocked appraisal absorbed the width of his bare brown shoulders above the sheet. Instantly she knew that he wasn't wearing a stitch.

'This bed was busier than the Rialto at high season last night,' Luca remarked.

'Zia needed the security of being with me. She was too cranky to settle somewhere strange on her own,' Darcy rushed to inform him, heart banging violently against her breastbone as she collided with flaring eyes as bright as shafts of golden sunlight in that lean, dark, devastating face.

'Were the dogs insecure too?'

'They cried at the door, Luca! They were really pathetic…'

'I wonder if I should have tried getting down on all fours and howling. I could have pretended to be a werewolf,' Luca suggested, taking advantage of her confusion to snake out an imprisoning arm and hold her where she was before she could go into sudden retreat. 'Then you would've had every excuse to tie me to the bed again.'

Darcy turned a slow hot crimson. Every inch of skin above the collar of her pyjama top was infiltrated by that sweeping tide of burning colour. *Again!* That single word was like a depth charge plunging into her memory banks to cause the maximum chaos. And, worst of all, he was exaggerating. With the aid of his bow tie, she had only got as far as anchoring one wrist before laughter had got the better of her dramatic intentions.

'Speaking as a male who until that night had never, ever relinquished control in the bedroom, I was delightfully surprised by your creativity—'

'I was *drunk!*' Darcy hissed in anguished self-defence.

'With a passionate desire to live out every fantasy you had ever had. Yes, you told me,' Luca reminded her without remorse as he leant over her and long fingers flicked loose the button at her throat without her noticing. 'You also told me that I was your dream lover…and you were undeniably mine. I don't have dream aspirations, but what I didn't know I was missing, I had in abundance that night, and since then no other woman has managed to satisfy me.'

'You're not serious,' Darcy mumbled shakily, mesmer-ised by the blaze of that golden gaze holding her own.

'So that is why you are here,' Luca confided with husky exactitude. 'I want to know *why* I find you so tormentingly attractive when my intelligence tells me that you are full of flaws.'

'Flaws?'

'You don't give a damn about your appearance. You're untidy, disorganised and blunt to the point of insanity. You hack wood like a lumberjack and you let dogs sleep on my bed. And, strange as it is, I have to confess that none of those habits or failings has the slightest cooling effect on my libido...' Lowering his imperious dark head on that admission, Luca skimmed aside the loose-cut pyjama top to press his mouth hotly to the tiny pulse flickering beneath the delicate skin of her throat.

'*Oh...*what are you doing?' Darcy yelped.

Involuntarily immobilised by the startling burst of warmth igniting low in her belly, she gazed up apprehen-sively at Luca as he lifted his head.

'Don't do that again,' she muttered weakly, her voice failing to rise to the command level required for the occa-sion. 'It makes me feel peculiar and we have to talk about things—'

'What sort of things?' Luca enquired thickly.

'That wretched ring for a start—'

'*No.*'

'I didn't steal it, Luca! And you should be trying to find out who *did!*' Darcy told him baldly.

His heated gaze cooled and hardened in the thumping silence.

Darcy gave him a weary, pleading look. 'I wouldn't *do* something like that...and as soon as I get home I'll be able to prove that the ring my father sold wasn't yours!'

'What do you hope to gain from these absurd lies and promises?' Luca demanded with raw impatience. 'I *know* that you took the Adorata! It is not remotely possible that anyone else could have carried out that theft. An idiot would confirm your guilt on less evidence than I have!'

'Circumstantial evidence, Luca...nothing more concrete.'

'While you refuse to admit the truth, there's nothing to discuss.' Luca studied her flushed and frustrated face with smouldering dark golden eyes. With cool deliberation, he smoothed the tumbled curls from her brow. 'All I want to do at this moment is make passionate love to you.'

'No!'

Luca let a teasing forefinger trail along the taut line of her mutinous lips, watched her shiver in shaken reaction to that contact. 'Even when you want to?'

'I don't want to!'

Suddenly alarmingly short of breath, Darcy looked back at him. Little prickles of tormenting awareness were filling her with tension. She was shamefully conscious of the raw, potent power of his abrasive masculinity, and of its devastating effect on her treacherous body. Already her breasts felt heavy and full, her nipples wantonly taut.

The silence pulsed.

'I *don't!* You think I'm a thief!' Darcy cried, as though he had argued with her.

Luca's smile was pure charisma unleashed. 'Possibly that's the most dangerous part of your attraction.'

Thoroughly disconcerted by that suggestion, Darcy frowned.

And, in a ruthless play on her bewilderment, Luca bent his well-shaped dark head and kissed her. He plundered her mouth like a warrior on the battlefield in a make-or-break encounter. She jerked as if fireworks were going off inside her. The hot, lustful thrust of his tongue electrified her. As she responded with all the answering hunger she could not suppress, nothing mattered to her but the continuance of that passionate assault.

In an indolent movement Luca sat up and carried her with him. He pushed the top down off her shoulders and trailed it free of her arms, freeing her hands to rise and sink into his luxuriant black hair. He released her reddened mouth, burnished golden eyes dropping lower to take in the tip-tilted curves of her small breasts and the bold thrust of her rosy nipples.

'You are so perfect,' he savoured huskily.

Perfect? *Never,* she thought, but in the pounding silence Darcy still found herself watching as he curved appreciative hands to her aching flesh. With a stifled moan, she shut her eyes tightly, but felt with every quivering fibre the shock-wave of shatteringly intense sensation as expert fingers toyed with the tender peaks. She trembled, her heartbeat thundering in her eardrums.

'*Dio…*' Luca drew in an audible breath. 'You always do exactly what excites me most…'

With a distinct lack of cool, he pushed her back against the pillows and closed his mouth urgently to the source of his temptation. As he tugged at the shamelessly engorged buds with erotic thoroughness she flung her head back, every muscle tensing as a low, keening sound of excitement escaped her. With every carnal caress he sent an arrow of shooting fire to the tormenting ache between her trembling thighs.

Her fingers knotted tightly into the glossy thickness of his hair, holding him to her, desperately urging him on. A moan of impatience left her lips as he abandoned her breasts to tug up her knees and free her restive lower limbs from the pyjama bottoms.

'Kiss me,' she muttered feverishly then.

'Want me?' Shimmering golden eyes welded to her darkened gaze and the longing she couldn't hide from him. 'How much?'

'Luca…' she whispered pleadingly, shivering with need.

'I find you incredibly sexy, *cara mia.*'

Rising over her, he slid a lean, hair-roughened thigh between hers and crushed her mouth with passionate fervour under his. There was no room for thought in her head.

Passion controlled her utterly. Her body writhed beneath his, a flood of hungry fire burning at the very heart of her. Feeling the bold promise of his manhood pulsing against her hip, she pushed against him in instinctive encouragement.

Luca pulled back from her, eyes smoky with desire. 'You're too impatient…the pleasure is all the keener when you wait for what you want. And didn't you make me wait that night?' A tantalising hand slowly smoothed over the tense muscles of her stomach. He listened to her suck in oxygen in noisy gasps of anticipation. 'In fact, you pushed me right over the edge when I was least expecting it.'

Instantly she was lost in that imagery. Luca, helpless in her thrall, driven to satisfaction against his own volition, disconcerted, reacting by suddenly reasserting his masculine dominance and driving her crazy with desire. She reached up to him, finding his sensual mouth again for herself, parting her lips to the stabbing invasion of his tongue. He shuddered violently against her, his control slipping as he kissed her back with raw, hungry force.

His hand skated through the damp auburn curls crowning the apex of her thighs and discovered the satin sensitivity of the moist flesh beneath. Mastered by a need that overwhelmed every restraint, she felt her spine arch, her body opening to him as the terrible ache for satisfaction blazed up, making her whimper and writhe, hungrily craving what he had taught her to crave in a torment of excitement.

'When you respond like that, all I can think about is plunging inside you,' Luca groaned, sliding between her thighs.

The hot, hard thrust of his powerful penetration took her breath away. Nothing had ever felt so good. Her whole being was centred on the feel of him inside her, boldly stretching and filling, and giving such intense pleasure she would have died had he stopped.

'You told me I was absolutely brilliant at this,' Luca reminded her, gazing down at her with a staggering mixture of lust laced with reluctant amusement as he plunged deeper still and watched her eyes close on a wave of electrified and utterly naked pleasure. '''Gosh, you're incredibly good at this too...'' you said, in such surprise. I wondered if you were going to score my technique on a questionnaire afterwards—'

'Shut up!' Darcy moaned with effort.

'You said that too.'

She stared up at him, at a peak of such extraordinary excitement she was ready to kill him if he didn't move.

And Luca vented a hoarse laugh. He *knew* how she felt. And his own struggle to maintain control was etched in his taut cheekbones, the sheen of sweat on his dark skin and the ragged edge to his voice. With a muffled groan of urgent satisfaction, he drove deeper into her yielding body. Her heart almost burst with the force of her own frantic response.

Mindless, she clung to him as he took her with a wild vigour that destroyed any semblance of control. Her release brought an electrifying explosion. As the paroxysms of uncontrollable pleasure overpowered her, her nails raked down his damp, muscular back. Luca cried out her name and shuddered over her, as lost in that world of physical sensation as she was.

The most unearthly silence reigned in the aftermath of that impassioned joining.

Luca disentangled himself and rolled over to a cooler part of the bed. Darcy stared fixedly at the footboard. Even before the last quakings of sated desire and intense pleasure faded, she felt rejected.

So you slept with him, a little voice said inside her blitzed brain. Did you do it to make this a real marriage that couldn't be annulled? Did you do it to hang onto the Folly? Or did you do it because you just couldn't summon up sufficient will-power to resist him? After all, you knew how fantastic he would be.

Darcy flipped her tousled head over to one side to anxiously scan Luca. He looked back at her, his strikingly handsome face taut but uninformative, expressive eyes screened. Darcy's throat closed over. At that moment she wanted very, very badly to believe that she had sacrificed her body for the sake of her home. It might have been a morally indefensible move, but her pride could have lived with such a cold-blooded decision...

It would be an infinitely greater challenge to co-exist with the ghastly knowledge that she had made love with Luca because she found him totally and absolutely irresistible, even when she ought to hate him...but, unhappily for her, that was the dreadful truth. And any denial of the fact would be complete cowardice.

It was equally craven to lie in the presence of the enemy behaving like a victim, drowning in defeat and loss of face. Darcy flinched from an image infinitely more shameful to her than any loss of control in Luca's arms. It was unthinkable to let Luca guess that making love with him could reduce her to such a turmoil of painful vulnerability.

'Right,' Darcy said flatly, galvanised into action by that awareness and abruptly sitting up with what she hoped was a cool, calm air of decision. 'Now that we've got *that* out of the way, perhaps we can talk business.'

*'Business?'* Luca stressed in sharp disconcertion, complete incredulity flaring in his brilliant dark eyes.

# CHAPTER EIGHT

'BUSINESS,' Darcy confirmed steadily.

'We have no mutual business interests to discuss,' Luca delivered rather drily.

'That's where you're wrong.' Her eyes gleamed at that dismissive assurance. 'As you were so eager to point out yesterday, the Folly estate is still on the brink of bankruptcy.' She breathed in deep. 'I only married you because I assumed that my bank manager would increase my overdraft limit once I explained to him about my godmother's will. However…he refused.'

From beneath dense ebony lashes, Luca surveyed her with something akin to unholy fascination.

'So as things stand,' Darcy recounted tautly, 'not only am I in no position to re-employ the staff laid off after my father's death, but I am also likely to have my home repossessed before that six months is even up.'

'One small question,' Luca breathed in a slightly strained undertone. He was now engaged on a fixed surveillance of the elaborate plasterwork on the ceiling above. 'Did you happen to mention my name to your bank manager?'

'What would I have mentioned your name for?' Darcy countered impatiently. 'I told him that I'd got married but that my husband would be having nothing to do with the estate.'

'Honesty is wonderful, but not always wise,' Luca remarked reflectively. 'I doubt that you need worry about any imminent threat of repossession. If you're only a little behind on the mortgage repayments, it's unlikely.'

'I disagree. I've had some very nasty letters on the subject already. Heavens, I'm scared to open my post these days!' Darcy admitted ruefully, thrusting bright curls from her troubled brow.

'Tell me, in a roundabout, extremely clumsy way, is it possible that you are trying to work yourself up to asking *me* for a loan?' Luca enquired darkly.

'Where on earth did you get that idea? I wouldn't touch your money with a barge-pole!' Darcy told him in indignant rebuttal. 'But I *need* to go home to visit all the other financial institutions that might help. I have to find somewhere prepared to invest in the future of the Folly!'

Luca now surveyed her with thunderous disbelief. 'That's a joke…isn't it?'

'Of course it's not a joke!' Darcy grimaced at the idea. 'Why would I joke about something so serious?'

As Luca sat up in one sudden powerful movement the sheet fell away from his magnificent torso. Outrage blazed in his dark eyes, his lean features clenched taut. 'Are you out of your tiny mind?' he roared back at her, making her flinch in shock from such unexpected aggression. 'I'm an extremely wealthy man…and as *my wife,* you dare to tell me that you plan to drag the Raffacani name in the dirt by scuttling round the banking fraternity begging for a *loan?* Are you trying to make me a laughing-stock?'

Darcy gazed back at him in stunned immobility. That possibility hadn't occurred to her. Nor, at that instant, would the prospect have deprived her of sleep.

'*Accidenti…*' Luca swore rawly, thrusting back the sheet and springing lithely from the bed to appraise her with diamond-hard eyes of condemnation. 'I now see that I have found a foe worthy of my mettle! You are one cunning little vixen! And if you dare put one foot inside the door of *any* financial institution, I will throw you out of my life the same day!'

A foe worthy of his mettle? An unearned compliment, Darcy conceded abstractedly, her attention wholly entrapped by the glorious spectacle of Luca striding naked up and down the bedroom with clenched fists of fury. Gosh, he was gorgeous. Glossy black hair, fabulous bone structure, eyes of wonderful vibrance. Broad shoulders, powerful chest, slim hips, long, long legs. The whole encased in wonderful golden skin, adorned with muscles and intriguing patches of black curly hair. All male.

She looked away, cheeks hot, shame enfolding her. She was so physically infatuated with the man she couldn't even concentrate on arguing with him. It was utterly disgusting.

'OK,' Luca snarled, further provoked by that seemingly stony and defiant silence. 'This is the deal. *I* will take over temporary responsibility for all bills relating to the Folly estate!'

Shaken by so unexpected not to mention so unwelcome a suggestion, Darcy turned aghast eyes on him. '*No way*...why would you want to do that?'

'I don't want to...but that arrangement would be preferable to placing an open chequebook into those hot, greedy little hands of yours! *Porca miseria!*' Luca shot her an intimidating glower of angry derision. 'The bedsheets are not even cooled before you start trying to rip me off again!'

He had a mind as complex as a maze, Darcy conceded, lost in wonder at such involved logic. He was so incredibly suspicious of her motives. All she had tried to do was stress how very urgently she needed to return home to sort out those problems with the estate, but Luca had flown off on another tangent entirely. He honestly believed that she had just tried to blackmail him. Admittedly, it should have dawned on her that he might be sensitive to the idea of his wife seeking to borrow money when he himself was filthy rich, but the reason it hadn't dawned on her was that she didn't feel remotely married to him.

'I don't want your rotten money...I've already told you that.'

'*Dio mio*...you will not seek to borrow anywhere else!' Luca asserted fiercely.

'That's not fair,' Darcy protested.

'Who ever said that I would be fair?'

'You did....' Darcy said in a small voice.

Luca froze at the reminder.

An electrifying silence stretched.

'Suddenly I have a great need for the calm, ordered atmosphere of my office!' Luca bit out with scantily controlled savagery. He strode into the bathroom and sent the door crashing shut.

So that's the temper...*wow!*

The door flew open again. 'Even in bed, don't you ever think of anything but that bloody house?' Luca flung, in final sizzling attack.

The door closed again.

*Wow*...Darcy thought again helplessly. He's so passionate when he drops the cool front. He slams doors like I do. He's a suspicious toad, so used to wheeling and dealing he can't take anything at face value. But he also thought she had put one over on him, she registered. The beginnings of a rueful smile tugged at the tense, unhappy line of her mouth.

What was the matter with her? she questioned as she slid out of bed. Why was she thinking such crazy thoughts? Why did she feel sort of disappointed that Luca was planning to leave her? Why wasn't she feeling more cheerful at that prospect? She stared down at the empty chair where she had draped her clothes the night before. With a frown, she finally noticed that her open suitcase had disappeared as well. She wandered into the dressing room and tugged open the unit doors to be greeted by male apparel on one side and on the other unfamiliar female garments.

Pyjama-clad, she knocked on the bathroom door. No answer. She opened it. He was in the shower.

'Where are my clothes, Luca?' she called.

The water went off. He rammed back the doors of the shower cubicle.

'I got rid of them,' Luca announced, raking an impatient hand through his dripping black hair and snatching up a towel.

'*Rid* of them?'

'Rather drastic, I know, but surely not a sacrifice?' Luca gave her an expectant look. 'Since you need lessons on how to dress. *Porca miseria!*' He grimaced, watched her face pale and telegraph hurt disbelief. 'That was tactless. But I just thought it would be easiest if I simply presented you with a new wardrobe. The clothes are in the dressing room. You won't even need to go shopping now.'

Darcy's eyes prickled with hot, scratchy tears. She was appalled. Never had she felt more mortified. This was a member of the opposite sex telling her she looked absolutely awful in her own clothes, telling her that *he,* a man, knew more than she did about how she should be dressing. 'How could you do that to me?' she gasped strickenly, and fled.

'It's a gift…a *surprise*…most women would be over the moon!' Luca fired back accusingly.

'Insensitive pig!' A sob tearing at her throat, Darcy threw herself back on the bed.

The mattress beside her gave with his weight.

'You have a beautiful face and an exquisite slender shape…but your clothes are all wrong,' Luca breathed huskily.

Darcy was humiliated and outraged by such smooth bare-faced lying. *She* knew better than anyone that she wasn't remotely beautiful! Flipping over in a blind fury, she raised her hand and dealt him a stinging slap.

'*Not*…most…women,' Luca muttered half under his breath, like somebody learning a very difficult lesson. With a slightly dazed air, he pressed long, elegant fingers to the flaming imprint of her fingers etched across one hard cheekbone and blinked.

Instantly, Darcy crumbled with guilt. 'I'm sorry…I shouldn't have done that,' she muttered brokenly. 'But you asked for it…you provoked me…go away!'

'I don't understand you—'

'I *hate* you…do you understand that?'

Darcy coiled away from him. She hurt so much inside she wanted to scream to let the pain out. She hugged herself tight. When Luca put a hand on her shoulder, she twisted violently away. When he reached for one of her hands, she shook him off.

'I actually liked you before I realised who you were!' she suddenly slung at him in disgust. 'I actually *trusted* you! Gosh, I've got great taste in men!'

'Haven't you already got what you wanted from me?' Luca raked back at her in cold anger. 'I have promised you my financial backing for the duration of our marriage. Your problems are over.'

Darcy regarded him with bitter outrage. 'I'm not something you can buy with your money.'

Luca shot her an icy unimpressed appraisal. 'If you're not…what are you doing in my bed?'

There was no answer to that question. She couldn't even explain that to her own satisfaction, never mind his. And that he should throw her sexual surrender in her face made her curl up and die deep down inside.

She listened to him dressing, and she was so quiet she barely breathed.

Luca forced himself under her notice again by coming to a halt two feet from the bed. Clad in a lightweight beautifully cut pearl-grey suit, he looked absolutely stupendous, but icily remote and intimidating…like someone who ate debtors five to a plate for breakfast. But now she knew that his black hair felt like silk when she smoothed her fingers through it, that his smile was like hot sunlight after the winter and that even his voice trickled down her spine like honey and made her melt, she thought in growing agony.

'This is not how I thought things would be with us. I'm civilised…I'm very civilised,' Luca informed her with unfeeling cool. 'We're supposed to be skimming along the surface of things and having a great time in bed. So tell me who bought the Adorata ring and we'll get that little complication out of the way. Then there is hope that peace will break out.'

'I've already told you that I did not take that ring,' Darcy whispered shakily.

'And repetition of that claim has an excessively aggravating effect on my normally even temper,' Luca drawled. 'We're at an impasse.'

Darcy studied him, cold fascination holding her tight but pain piercing her like cutting shards of glass—that same pain bright and unconcealed in her eyes. 'I can't believe that you're the same guy I met three years ago...I can't believe that we laughed and danced and you were just so romantic and warm and—'

'*Stupid?*' Luca slotted in glacially, deep-set dark eyes hard as diamonds but a feverish flush accentuating the taut slant of his high cheekbones. 'Absurd? Ridiculous? After all, outside my own élite circle, I wasn't streetwise enough to protect myself from a calculating little predator like you!'

Darcy was shaken by that response, dredged from her own self-preoccupation to finally think about how *he* must have felt when he'd believed he had been robbed by the woman he had spent the previous evening romancing in high style, the woman he had brought into his home, the woman he had made love to over and over again until they'd fallen asleep in each other's arms. And for the very first time she recognised the raw, angry bitterness he had until now contrived to conceal from her. He was very proud, hugely self-assured. The discovery that the ring had gone could scarcely have failed to dent his male ego squarely where it hurt most. Heavens, what an idiot he must have felt, she registered, with a belated flood of understanding sympathy.

'Luca...' she breathed awkwardly. 'I—'

Luca vented a harsh laugh. 'You were clever, but not clever enough,' he murmured with a grim twist of his mouth. 'I *was* a very conservative guy. I was twenty-eight and I had never felt anything very much for any woman. But with you I felt something special—'

'S-something special?' Darcy broke in helplessly.

Derision glittered in the look he cast her intent face. 'You could have got so much more out of me than one night if you'd stayed around.'

'I don't think so,' Darcy whispered unevenly, desperately wanting to be convinced to the contrary. 'I was playing Cinderella that night.'

'Cinderella left her slipper behind…she didn't crack open the Prince's safe.'

'But it wasn't *real*…those hours we spent together,' she continued shakily, still praying that he would tell her different, and all because he had said those two words 'something special'. 'You said all the right lines; I succumbed… Yes, well, maybe I more than succumbed. I guess I was a bit more active than that, but you had no intention of ever seeing me again…' She shrugged a slight shoulder jerkily, no longer able to meet his shrewd gaze, and plucked abstractedly at the sheet. 'I mean…I mean, *obviously* you never had the smallest intention of showing up on the Ponte della Guerra the next day.'

'You remember that?' Luca said, with the kind of surprise that suggested he was amazed that she should have recalled something so trivial.

Darcy remembered standing on that bridge for hours, and she could have wept at the memory. If there ever had been a chance that he would turn up, there had been none whatsoever after he had realised that he'd been robbed that same night. So it was all *his* fault. All her agonies could be laid at his door. And why was she thinking like this anyway? He couldn't possibly find her beautiful. Though he had behaved as if he did that night. True, she had looked really well, but surely his standards of female beauty had to be considerably higher?

'I have bright red hair,' Darcy remarked stiltedly.

'I could hardly miss the fact, but it's not mere red, it's

Titian, and I'd prefer to see a lot more of it,' Luca proffered after some hesitation.

'But you must've noticed that I have a...a snub nose?'

'Retroussé is the word...it's unusual; it adds distinction to your face... Why am I having this weird conversation with you?' Luca demanded freezingly. He strode to the door, glanced grudgingly back over one broad shoulder. 'I'll see you later.'

Emptied of his enervating presence, the room seemed dim and dull.

But Darcy lay where she was. Luca liked her nose; he liked her hair. What everybody else called skinny, he called 'slender'. Strange taste, but she knew she wouldn't have the heart to tell him that. So Luca, who resembled her every fantasy of physical male perfection, could get the hots for a skinny redhead with a snub nose. That fact was a revelation to Darcy. No wonder he was annoyed with himself, but all of a sudden she wasn't annoyed with him at all.

He hadn't made love to her just out of a desire for revenge. No, he wasn't as self-denying as that. Luca had really *wanted* to make love to her. There was nothing false about his desire for her. Everything he had said in bed must have been the truth...even the part about no other woman being able to satisfy him since?

Something special? Why did she feel so forgiving all of a sudden? Why was her brain encased in a fog of confusing emotion? That wretched, hateful ring that had been stolen, she reflected grimly. Take that problem out of their relationship and how might Luca behave then? But even if she contrived that miracle, exactly how would he react to the news that the toddler from hell was *his* daughter?

It was early days yet, Darcy decided ruefully. A lot could happen in six months. Telling him that he had fathered a child the night of the ball might presently seem like an impressive counter-punch, but she didn't want to use Zia like a weapon in a battle which nobody could win. In fact, she conceded then, unless their marriage became a real marriage, she was pretty sure she would never tell Luca that Zia was his child. What would be the point?

Right now she had much more important things to consider: the Folly estate and how she planned to save it in the short-term. Borrowing money appeared to be out of the question. And accepting Luca's financial help would choke her. So was she going to have to steel herself to sell some of the Folly's glorious Tudor furniture at auction? If she did so, the pieces could never, ever be replaced. But what alternative way did she have of raising the cash to keep her home afloat over the next six months?

An hour later, garbed in a figure-hugging sapphire-blue dress and horrendously high stilettos, Darcy bent down with extreme caution to lift Zia up into her arms, and *bang*— inspiration hit her the same second that her attention fell on the glossy gossip magazine the middle-aged nursemaid had left lying on a nearby chair. Didn't people pay good money for an insight into the lives of the rich and famous? Wasn't Luca both rich and famous? And didn't she have a second cousin who was a secretary on one of those publications?

What would an interview and a few photos of Gianluca Raffacani's bride be worth?

Darcy blinked, cringing from the concept but hardening herself against a sensitivity she could no longer afford. Luca had said that infidelity or desertion would be grounds for ending their marital agreement. But he hadn't mentioned publicity...

# CHAPTER NINE

HAVING heard the commotion, Darcy rose from her seat in the drawing room and walked to the door that opened onto the vast reception hall. She froze there, taken aback by the scene being enacted before her startled eyes.

On his return home, Luca was being engulfed by his sister's dogs. It was like a rugby scrum. But astonishingly informative. Aristide and Zou Zou adored him, Darcy registered in surprise. And there he was, fondling shaggy ears and valiantly bearing up to the exuberant welcome he was receiving. Failing to notice her, Luca then took the stairs two at a time, a gift-wrapped package clutched in one hand.

Since Darcy was a very slow mover in the unfamiliar high heels, she didn't catch up with him. And she was perplexed when he strode past their bedroom to turn up the flight of stairs that led to the nursery suite. She came to a halt in the doorway of the playroom. By the time she got there, Zia had already ripped the paper off a box which she was now regarding with enraptured bliss.

'Dolly!' she gasped, squeezing the box so tight in her excitement that it crunched. 'Pretty dolly!'

Peer pressure and television had a lot to answer for, Darcy decided uncomfortably. All the other little girls Zia knew at the playgroup already had that doll, but Darcy had ignored all pleas to make a similar purchase. Why? Because that particular doll had always reminded her of Maxie. Now that seemed so inadequate an excuse when she saw Zia reacting like a deprived child suddenly shot into seventh heaven.

'Shall I take her out of the box?' Luca enquired helpfully.

While Zia pondered whether or not she could bear to part with her gift even briefly, Darcy studied Luca's hard, classic profile, which showed to even better advantage when he was smiling. She was frankly bewildered by what she was seeing.

Zia extended the box. Hunkering down on a level with the toddler, Luca removed the packaging and finally freed the soft-bodied version of the doll. '*See,* Mummy!' her daughter carolled with pride.

As Luca's well-shaped dark head whipped round to finally note Darcy's silent presence, Darcy reddened with awful self-consciousness beneath his lengthy appraisal. While unnecessarily engaged in smoothing down the skirt of her dress with damp palms, she strove to act unconcerned and evaded his scrutiny. 'Did you say thank you, Zia?'

'Kiss?' Zia proffered instantly, moving forward to land a big splashy kiss on Luca's cheek and then give him an enthusiastic hug.

'Isn't cupboard love great?' Luca mocked his own calculation with an amused smile and vaulted upright again. 'We got off on the wrong foot yesterday. A peace offering was a necessity.'

'It was a kind thought,' Darcy conceded stiltedly.

'I can be very kind, *bella mia,*' Luca countered huskily.

Darcy collided with his scorching dark stare. And quite without knowing *how* she knew it, she knew he was thinking about sex. That sixth sense awareness spooked her and plunged her into confusion.

As her skin heated her breath caught in her throat, and her heart gave a violent lurch. She couldn't look away from those stunning dark golden eyes. The impact of that look was staggering. She felt dizzy, unsteady on her feet and far, far too hot. The tip of her tongue skimmed along her dry lower lip in a nervous motion. Luca's intent scrutiny homed in on the soft fullness of her mouth. Something drew tight and twisted, low in her stomach, a sexual response so powerful it terrified her. Mercifully, Zia broke the connection by holding out her new doll for her mother's admiration.

'You haven't much time to say goodnight to her. My sister is joining us for dinner,' Luca advanced as he strode out through the door. 'I need a shower and a change of clothes.'

'Night-night, Luca!' Zia called cheerfully.

Luca paused and glanced back with a raised ebony brow. 'In the right mood, she's really quite sweet, isn't she?' His eyes became shadowed and his wide mouth compressed. 'I had nothing to do with Ilaria when she was that age...I was at boarding school. She was only seven when I went to university. I lived to regret not having a closer bond with her.'

Twenty minutes later, having tucked Zia into bed and read her a story, Darcy walked into their bedroom. Only his jacket and tie removed, Luca was in the act of putting down his mobile phone.

'You look fantastic in that dress...you know why?' A wolfish grin slashed his lean, strong face. 'It *fits*. It isn't two sizes too large or a foot too long!'

'Margo always helped me to choose my clothes,' Darcy confided. 'She said that I had to dress to hide my deficiencies.'

'You have none. You're in perfect proportion for your size.'

But Darcy's diminutive curves and lack of height *had* been deficiencies to a stepmother who was both tall and lushly female in shape. Margo had loathed red hair as well, insisting that Darcy could only wear dull colours. Growing up with Margo's constant criticism, and Nina's pitying superiority, Darcy had learned only to measure her looks against theirs. That unwise comparison had wrecked her confidence in her own appearance.

But now she gazed back at Luca and could not fail to recognise his sincerity. He'd told her she looked fantastic. And sensual appreciation radiated from the lingering appraisal in those intent dark eyes. If she didn't yet quite credit that she *could* look fantastic, she certainly realised with a surge of gratified wonder that Luca genuinely *believed* she did.

Her softened gaze ran with abstracted admiration over his long, lean, powerful physique. She was shaken to note the earthy and defiantly male thrust of arousal that the close fit of his well-cut trousers couldn't conceal. She reddened hotly, but she also felt empowered and outrageously feminine.

'Luca…' she whispered shakily.

Later, she couldn't recall who had reached out first. She remembered the way his gaze narrowed, the blaze of golden intent between black spiky lashes, and then suddenly she was crushed in his arms and clinging to him to stay upright. He parted her lips to invade her tender mouth with his thrusting tongue, dipping, twirling, tasting her with fierce, impatient need. He cut right through her every defence with that blunt, honest admission of desire. She trembled violently beneath that devouring kiss. He made her feel possessed, dominated, and utterly weak with hunger.

'I should never have left you…I've been in a filthy temper all day,' Luca confided raggedly, slumberous eyes scanning her lovely face with very male satisfaction, a febrile flush on his taut cheekbones. 'I want you *so* much…'

'Yes…' Darcy acknowledged a truth too obvious to be denied. She felt the same. Her heart was pounding, her whole body throbbing with intense arousal. It was like being in pain; it made her crave him like a drug.

'I can't wait until later…I'm in agony,' Luca gritted roughly.

Hard fingers splayed across her spine to press her into direct contact with his hard thighs. He shuddered against her with a stifled groan, kissing her temples, the top of her head, running his fingers through her hair and then bringing her mouth back hungrily under his again. She couldn't get close enough to him. He slid one hand beneath her skirt, skimming up a slender thigh to the very heart of her. The damp swollen heat of her beneath the thin barrier of her panties betrayed her response. Excitement made her squirm and moan against that skilled touch.

'Luca...*please*,' she gasped urgently.

He backed her down on the side of the bed. He leant over her, hands braced on either side of her head, and plunged deep into her mouth again, eliciting a low cry of surrender from her. Tugging down the zip on her dress, he removed it, skimming off her remaining garments with deft, impatient hands. He stilled for a second, reverent eyes scanning the pouting curves of her breasts and the silky dark red hair at the apex of her slender thighs.

'You are gorgeous, *bella mia*...how can you ever have doubted that?' Luca demanded as he stood over her, peeling off his own clothing at speed.

He came down to her, gloriously aroused. Cupping her breasts, he caressed the sensitive buds with his lips and his tongue, and then he kissed a slow tantalising trail down over the flexing muscles of her stomach, pushing her quivering thighs apart to conduct a more intimate exploration. She was shocked, but too tormented by her own aching need for his caresses to stop him. He controlled her utterly, pushed her to such a pitch of writhing, desperate excitement she was helpless.

He rose over her again, his breathing fractured. He dipped his tongue between her reddened lips in a sexy flick as he tipped back her thighs with almost clumsy hands, his own excitement palpable. Burnished golden eyes assailed hers. He hesitated at the crucial moment when she was braced for the hot, hard invasion of his body into hers.

'Luca!'

'*Dio mio*...I don't know myself like this!' he groaned ruefully. 'I feel wild...but I don't want to hurt you.'

'You won't...'

'You're so much smaller than I am.'

'I like it when you're wild,' she whispered feverishly.

Above her, Luca closed his eyes and slammed into her hard, releasing such a flood of electrifying sensation that Darcy moaned his name like a benediction. He withdrew and entered her again, with a raw, forceful sense of timing that was soul-shatteringly effective. Her entire being was centred on the explosive pleasure building inside her. Heart pounding in concert with his, she cried out in ecstasy as he drove her over the edge. Then she just collapsed, totally drained.

They lay together in a sweaty huddle. Luca released her from his weight but retained a possessive hold on her, pressing his mouth softly to her throat, lingering to lick the salt from her skin and smooth a soothing hand down over her slender back.

'That was unbelievable…that was paradise, *cara mia*,' Luca sighed in a tone of wondering satisfaction. 'I have never felt this good.'

'What time is your sister coming?' Darcy mumbled.

Luca tensed, relocated the wrist with a watch, and suddenly wrenched himself free. '*Porca miseria*…Ilaria will be here at any moment!'

Feeling totally brainless and lethargic, Darcy watched him spring off the bed.

'Darcy…' he gritted then.

'What?' she whispered with a silly smile, surveying him with a kind of bursting feeling inside her heart.

'You can share my shower.' Luca scooped her up into his powerful arms and strode into the bathroom with her.

'I'll never get my hair dry!' But still she watched him, trying desperately hard to work out why she felt so ecstatically happy.

'Your eyes are glowing like neon lights.' Studying her with a curiously softened look in his dark, deep-set gaze, Luca hooked her arms round his strong brown throat and kissed her again, holding her plastered to every inch of him beneath the gushing cascade of water. He raised his head again, a slight frown drawing his black brows together. 'I assume you're on the pill...'

'Nope.'

'I didn't use anything to protect you,' Luca told her slowly as he lowered her back down to the floor of the cubicle. '*Santo cielo*...how could I be that careless?'

Darcy had stiffened. How could *she* be that careless *again?* Yet another time. The first occasion had resulted in Zia's conception. She had foolishly assumed that the course of contraceptive pills she had stopped taking the day she failed to marry Richard would still prevent a pregnancy. Naturally it hadn't. Her own ignorance had been her downfall.

'Very little risk,' she muttered awkwardly, avoiding his searching scrutiny.

'You would know that better than I.'

He was wrong there, Darcy conceded ruefully. Her monthly cycles caused her so little inconvenience that she never bothered to keep a note of dates. She hadn't a clue what part of her cycle she was in, but she had almost supernatural faith in the power of Luca's fertility. Suppose she did become pregnant again... Oddly enough, the prospect failed to rouse the slightest sense of alarm. Indeed, as Darcy looked up at Luca, mentally miles away while he washed her, she was picturing a small boyish version of those same features that distinguished Zia. A buoyant warm sensation instantly blossomed inside her. Only when she appreciated how she was reacting to that prospect of pregnancy was she shocked by herself.

'What's wrong?' Luca prompted.

In her haste to escape those frighteningly astute eyes, Darcy lurched out of the shower. Grabbing up a towel, she took refuge in the dressing room to dry herself. I can't be in love with him. I can't be, she told herself sickly. It was a kind of immature infatuation and it had its sad roots in the past. Karen had been right about her: she *had* spent too much time alone. Building romantic castles in the air around Luca Raffacani would be a very stupid move, and, having done it once and learnt her mistake, she was convinced she was too sensible to be so foolish again.

By one of those strange tricks of fate Luca found her attractive, and they were sexually compatible, but she would have to be an idiot to imagine that Luca might now develop some form of emotional attachment to her. He had said it himself only this morning, hadn't he? He had talked with outrageous unapologetic cool about how they should be 'skimming along the surface of things and having a great time in bed' rather than arguing. Suddenly Darcy was very glad she had slapped him so hard...

'Tell me about your sister,' Darcy invited Luca as they left the bedroom. Having donned an elegant black dress and fresh lingerie at speed, she had attempted to coax her damp curls into some semblance of a style, but she was out of breath and her cheeks were still pink with effort. 'It'll look strange if I know nothing about her.'

Luca, as sleek and cool and elegant as a male who had spent a leisurely hour showering, shaving and donning his superb dinner jacket and narrow black trousers, gave her a wry look. 'My parents died in a plane crash when Ilaria was eight. My aunt became her legal guardian. I was only nineteen. Emilia was a childless widow, eager to mother my sister, but she was very possessive. She made it difficult for me to maintain regular contact with Ilaria.'

'That was selfish of her.'

'She also refused to allow me to share in Ilaria's upbringing when I was in a position to offer her a more settled home life. And she was a very liberal guardian. She spoilt Ilaria rotten. When my sister turned into a difficult teenager, Emilia saw her behaviour as rank ingratitude. Being a substitute mother had become a burden. She demanded that I take responsibility for Ilaria and within the same month she moved to New York.'

'Oh, dear...' Darcy grimaced.

'Ilaria was devastated by that rejection and she furiously resented me. We had some troubled times,' Luca conceded with a rueful shrug. 'She's twenty now, but I have little contact with her. As soon as she reached eighteen, she demanded an apartment of her own.'

'I'm sorry.' Seeing his dissatisfaction with this detached state of affairs, Darcy rested her hand on his sleeve in a sympathetic gesture. 'I always think the worst wounds are inflicted within the family circle. We're all much more vulnerable where our own flesh and blood is concerned.'

'You're thinking of your father?'

'It's hard not to. I spent my whole life wanting to be *somebody* in his eyes, struggling to win his respect,' Darcy admitted gruffly.

'Everyone's like that with parents.'

Tensing as she noticed his attention dropping to the hand still curved to his arm, she hurriedly removed it, thinking then with pain that the kind of physical closeness which he was at ease with *in* bed seemed a complete no-no *out* of bed.

'But I was reaching for something I could never have. I don't think my father ever looked at me without resenting the fact that I wasn't the son he wanted...but all that made me do was try harder,' she confided ruefully.

Luca reached for her hand and curled lean fingers tautly round hers. 'Was that why you took the Adorata?' he demanded in a roughened undertone, shrewd dark eyes drawn to her startled face. 'Darcy impressively riding to the rescue of the family fortunes with a pretend lucky find?'

Caught unprepared, Darcy lost every scrap of colour in her cheeks, her green eyes darkening with hurt at that absurd suspicion. Once again she had forgotten what lay between them, and with too great a candour she had exposed herself to attack.

'You must've lied to your father. He may have been domineering and aggressive, but he had the reputation of being an honest, upright man. Did you tell him that you had found it in some dusty antique shop where you had bought it for a song?' Luca pressed with remorseless persistence.

A door opened off the ball. Both Darcy and Luca whipped round. A slim, stunning girl with shoulder-length dark hair and a sullen expression subjected them to a stony appraisal.

'I have no intention of wasting an entire evening waiting for you to show up at your own dinner table, Luca,' Ilaria said with brittle sarcasm. 'Just why did you bother to invite me?'

'I hoped that you might want to meet Darcy. I'm sorry that we've kept you waiting,' Luca murmured levelly.

Ilaria vented a thin laugh. 'Why didn't you give me the opportunity to meet her *before* you got married?'

'I left several messages on your answering machine. You never call back,' Luca countered calmly.

The combination of aggression and hurt emanating from Ilaria was powerful. But then her big brother had married a total stranger. In those circumstances, her hostility was natural, Darcy conceded. Tugging free of Luca, she walked over to his sister, a rueful look of appeal in her eyes. 'You have every right to be furious. And I don't know how to explain why—'

'We got married in a hurry,' Luca slotted in with finality as he thrust open the door of the dining room. Atmospheric pools of candlelight illuminated the beautifully set table awaiting them. 'There's not much else to say.'

'I can't imagine you doing anything in a hurry without good reason, Luca,' Ilaria gibed. 'Have you got her pregnant?'

Darcy froze, and then forced herself down into the seat Luca had spun out for her occupation. While Luca shot a low-pitched sentence of icy Italian at his sister, Darcy drowned in guilty pink colour and glanced at neither combatant. The suggestion had been chosen to insult, but it was more apt than either of her companions could know.

However, she recognised the position Luca had put himself in, and she wanted to help minimise the damage to his already strained relationship with his sister.

'We had a quiet wedding because my father died recently.' Darcy spoke up abruptly. 'I have to admit that we were rather impulsive—'

'Impulsive? *Luca?*' Ilaria derided, unimpressed. 'Who do you think you're kidding? He never makes a single move that he hasn't planned down to the last detail!'

'In this case, he did,' Darcy persisted quietly. 'But it was selfish of us to just rush off and get married without letting our families share in the event.'

'Your family wasn't there *either?*' The younger woman looked astonished, but was visibly soothed by the admission. 'So where did you meet…and when?'

'That's a long story—' Luca began.

Darcy rushed to interrupt him. Telling the truth, or as much of it as was reasonable, would be wisest in the circumstances, rather than that silly story of her having reversed into his car in London and shouted at him. This *was* his sister they were dealing with, and Ilaria had to know that Luca would have wiped the pavement with any female that stupid.

'I met your brother almost three years ago at a masked ball here,' Darcy admitted, an anxious smile on her lips.

The effect of that simple statement stunned Darcy. To her left, Luca released his breath in a stark hiss and shot her a look of outright exasperation. To her right, Ilaria's face locked tight. She gaped at Darcy in the most peculiar way, her mouth a shocked and rounded circle from which no sound emitted, her olive skin draining to a sick pallor which made her horrified dark eyes look huge.

'I seem to have—'

'Put a giant foot in your mouth,' Luca completed grimly.

And then everything went crazy. Just as Darcy realised with a sinking heart that naturally his sister had to be aware of the theft that had taken place that night, and that she had just foolishly exposed Luca and herself to the need for an explanation that would be wellnigh impossible to make, Ilaria flew upright. The focus of her stricken attention was surprisingly not Darcy, but her brother.

As Ilaria began ranting hysterically at Luca in Italian she backed away from the table. A look of astonished incomprehension on his taut features, Luca rose upright and strode towards his sister. '*Cosa c'e che non va...*what's wrong?' he demanded urgently, anxiously.

Crying now in earnest, Ilaria clumsily evaded her brother's attempt to place comforting hands on her shoulders. Tearing herself away, she gasped out something in her own language and fled.

Instead of following her, Luca froze there as if his sister had struck him. He raised his lean hands, spread them slightly in an odd, inarticulate movement, and then slowly dropped them again.

Darcy hurried over to his side. 'What's the matter with her?'

His clenched profile starkly delineated against the flickering pools of shadow and light, Luca drew in a deep, shuddering breath. He turned a strange, unfocused look on Darcy. 'She said...she *said*...' he began unevenly.

'She said...*what?*' Darcy prompted impatiently, listening to Ilaria having a rousing bout of hysterics in the hall.

'Ilaria said *she* stole the Adorata ring,' Luca finally got out, and he shook his glossy dark head in so much shock and lingering disbelief he had the aspect of a very large statue teetering dangerously on its base.

'Oh...*oh, dear,*' Darcy muttered, so shaken by that shattering revelation that she couldn't for the life of her manage to come up with anything more appropriate.

Ilaria was sobbing herself hoarse in the centre of the hall. Darcy tried to put her arms round the girl and got pushed away. Ilaria shot an accusing, gulping stream of Italian at her.

'I'm sorry, but I was absolutely lousy at languages at

school.' Darcy curved a determined hand round the girl's
elbow and urged her into the drawing room. 'I know you're
very upset...but try hard to calm down just a *bit*,' she
pleaded.

'How can I? Luca will never forgive me!' Ilaria wailed,
and she flung herself face-down on a sofa to sob again.

Sitting down beside her, Darcy let her cry for a while.
But as soon as Luca entered the room she got up and said
awkwardly, 'Look...I'll leave you two alone—'

'No!' Ilaria suddenly reached out to grab at Darcy's
hand. 'You stay...'

'Yes...because if you don't, Darcy,' Luca muttered in
the strangest tone of eerie detachment from his sister's distress, 'I may just kill her.'

'You're nearly as bad as she is!' Darcy condemned
roundly as Ilaria went off into another bout of tormented
sobbing. 'You won't get any sense out of her talking like
that.'

'I know very well how to get sense out of her!'

Luca rapped out a command in staccato Italian which
sounded very much like a version of pull-yourself-together-
or-*else*.

'I'm sorry...I'm really s-sorry!' Ilaria gulped brokenly
then. 'I panicked when I realised that Darcy was the woman
you met that night... Because you had *married* her I
thought you had guessed...and that you had brought me
over here to confront me with what I did!'

'Your brother wouldn't behave like that,' Darcy said quietly.

Luca shot her a curious, almost pained look, and then
turned his attention back to his sister. 'How did you do it?'

'You shouldn't have been at the apartment at all that
evening because it was the night of the ball.' Sitting bolt-
upright now on the sofa, clutching the tissue that Darcy had
fetched for her use, Ilaria began to shred it with restive,
trembling hands. 'I needed money and you'd cut off my
allowance...refused to let me even see Pietro...I was so

*angry* with you! I was going to run away with him, but we needed money to do that—'

'You were seventeen,' Luca cut in harshly. 'I did what I had to do to protect you from yourself. If you hadn't been an heiress that sleazy louse wouldn't have given you a second glance!'

'Let her tell her story,' Darcy murmured, watching Ilaria cringe at that blunt assessment.

'I h-had a key to the apartment. I knew all the security codes. One day when I had lunch there with you, you went into the safe and I watched you do it from the hall,' Ilaria mumbled shamefacedly. 'I thought there would be cash in the safe...'

'Your timing was unfortunate.'

'All there was...was the Adorata,' Ilaria continued shakily. 'I was furious, so I took it. I told myself I was entitled to it if I needed it, but when I took the Adorata to Pietro, he...he laughed in my face! He said he wasn't fool enough to try and sell a famous piece of stolen goods. He said he would have had Interpol chasing him across Europe in pursuit of it...so I planned to put the ring back the next morning.'

'That was a timely change of heart,' Darcy put in encouragingly, although one look at Luca's icily clenched and remote profile reduced her to silence again.

'But you see, you went back to the apartment that night and stayed there...you found the safe open and the Adorata gone...I was too *late!*' Ilaria wailed.

'What did you do with the ring?'

'It's safe,' his sister hastened to assure him. 'It's in my safety deposit box with Mamma's jewellery.'

Momentarily, Luca closed his eyes at that news. *'Porca miseria...'* he ground out unsteadily. 'All this time...'

'If you'd called in the police I would have had to tell you I had it,' his sister muttered, almost accusingly. 'But when I realised you believed that the woman you'd left the ball with had taken it...' She shot a severely embarrassed glance at Darcy, belatedly recalling that that woman and her brother's wife were now one and the same. 'I mean—'

'*Me*…it's all right,' Darcy cut in, but her cheeks were burning.

'You see…' Ilaria hesitated. 'You weren't like a real person to me, and it didn't seem to matter who Luca blamed as long as he didn't suspect me.'

Darcy studied the exquisite Aubusson carpet fixedly, mortification overpowering her. She could well imagine how low an opinion Ilaria must have had of her at seventeen: some tramp who had dived into bed with her brother the same night she had first met him.

Disconcertingly, Luca vented a flat, humourless laugh. 'Aren't you fortunate that Darcy disappeared into thin air?'

Darcy was more than willing to disappear into thin air all over again. She turned towards the door. 'I think you need to talk without a stranger around,' she said with a rather tremulous smile.

Distinctly shaky after the strain of the scene she had undergone, Darcy shook her head apologetically at Luca's manservant, who was now hovering uncomfortably in the dining room doorway, obviously wondering what was happening and whether or not any of them intended to sit down and eat dinner like civilised people. She had enjoyed a substantial lunch earlier in the day and now she felt pretty queasy.

Poor Luca. Poor Ilaria. Such a shaming secret must have been horrible for the girl to live with for so long. A moment's reckless bitter rebellion over the head of some boy she had clearly been hopelessly infatuated with. As Ilaria matured that secret would have weighed ever more heavily on her conscience, probably causing her to assume a defensive attitude to cover her unease in Luca's presence.

Guilt did that—it ate away at you. Little wonder that Ilaria had avoided Luca's company. She had been too afraid to face up to what she had done and confess. And the instant Ilaria had appreciated that her brother's wife was also the woman Luca had once believed to be a thief, she had jumped to the panic-stricken conclusion that Luca somehow knew that *she* was the culprit. After all, how could Ilaria ever have guessed that her lordly big brother might have married a woman he *still* believed to be a thief out of a powerful need to punish her?

And now Luca would finally get that wretched ring back. Could he really believe that any inanimate object, no matter how valuable, precious and rare, was worth so much grief? How did he feel now that he knew he had misjudged her? Gutted, Darcy decided without hesitation. He had looked absolutely gutted when comprehension rolled over him like a drowning tidal wave. His *own* sister.

Darcy heaved a sigh. Maybe, as Luca had said himself, peace would now break out. Naturally he would have to apologise…in fact a bit of crawling wouldn't come amiss, Darcy thought, beginning to feel rather surprisingly upbeat. Having checked on Zia, she wandered downstairs again and into the dining room.

She sat down at the table, appetite restored, and tucked into her elaborate starter. No, she didn't want Luca to crawl. He was having a tough enough time with Ilaria and his spectacular own goal of misjudgement. She had to be fair. The evidence had been very much stacked against her. And how could he ever have suspected his seventeen-year-old sister of pulling off such a feat?

She was halfway through the main course when Luca appeared. '*Santo cielo*…how can you eat at a time like this?' he breathed in a charged tone of incredulity.

'I felt hungry…sorry to be so prosaic,' Darcy muttered, wondering where that rather melodramatic opening was about to take him. 'How's Ilaria?'

'I persuaded her to stay the night. I'm sorry about that…'

'About what?' Conscious that the sight of the cutlery still in her grasp seemed to be an offence of no mean order in his eyes, she abandoned her meal. In fact, in the mix of shadow and dim light in which Luca stood poised, the dark, sombre planes of his unusually pale features lent him an almost lost, lonely sort of aspect.

'About what?' Luca echoed, frowning as if he was struggling to get a grip on himself. 'Aren't you furious with Ilaria?'

'Gosh, no...she was terribly distressed. She's rather young for her age—very...well, emotional,' Darcy selected, striving to be tactful for once in her life.

'Being emotional is not catching...is it? You must be outraged with me,' Luca breathed starkly.

'Well, yes, I was when all this nonsense started—'

'*Nonsense?*' Luca cut in with ragged stress.

Darcy rose to her feet, wishing she could just run over and put her arms round him, spring him out of this strange and unfamiliar mood he was in, but he looked so incredibly remote now. As if he had lost everything he possessed. But he would strangle the first person who had the bad taste to either mention it or show a single hint of pity or understanding.

'I *always* knew I didn't take the wretched thing,' she pointed out gently. 'I'm awfully glad it's all cleared up now. And I understand why you were so convinced I was the thief...after all, you didn't *know* me, did you?'

Luca flinched as if she had punched him in the stomach. He spun his dark head away. 'No...I didn't,' he framed almost hoarsely.

She watched him swallow convulsively.

Feeling utterly helpless, craving the confidence to bridge the frightening gap she could feel opening up between them, Darcy was gripped by a powerful wave of frustration. He was so at a loss; she wanted to hug him the way she hugged Zia when she fell over and hurt herself. But she thought she would crack their tenuous relationship right down the middle if she made such an approach. He was too proud.

'We'll talk later,' Luca imparted with what sounded like

a really dogged effort to sound his usual collected self. 'You need to be alone for a while.'

*He* needed to be alone for a while, Darcy interpreted without difficulty. He's going to walk out on me...what did I do wrong? a voice screamed inside her bemused head. Here she was, being as fair, honest and reasonable as she knew how to be, and the wretched man was withdrawing more from her with every second.

'Tell me...would you have preferred a screaming row?'

'We have nothing to row about any more,' Luca countered, without a shade of his usual irony. In fact he sounded as if his only enjoyment in life had been wrenched from him by the cruellest of fates.

As the clock on the mantelpiece struck midnight, Darcy rose with a sigh. And that was when she heard the sound of footsteps in the hall. As the drawing room door opened, she tensed. For a split second Luca stilled at the sight of her, veiled eyes astutely reading the anxious, assessing look in hers.

'Would you like a drink?' he murmured quietly as he thrust the door closed.

'A brandy...' She watched him stride over to the ornate oriental drinks cabinet. Lithe, dark, strikingly good-looking, every movement fluid as poetry. He didn't look gutted any more—but then she hadn't expected him to. Luca was tough, a survivor, and survivors knew how to roll with the punches.

But *she* must have been born under an unlucky star. What savage fate had decreed that she should be involved up to her throat in the two biggest mistakes Luca had ever made? It was so cruel. He would judge himself harshly and he would never think of her without guilty unease again. She was like an albatross in his life, always a portent of doom. She hoved in to his radius and things went badly wrong. If he was like every other man she had ever known, he would very soon find the very sight of her an objectionable reminder of his own lowest moments.

Luca handed her the balloon glass of brandy, his lean, strong face sombre. 'I have come to some conclusions.'

Menaced by both expression and announcement, Darcy downed the brandy in one long, desperate gulp.

'You must have found the last few days very traumatic,' Luca breathed heavily, fabulous bone structure rigid. 'In retrospect, it is impossible to justify anything that I have done. I can make no excuse for myself; I can only admit that from the instant I found you gone from the apartment, the safe open, the Adorata gone, I nourished an obsessive need to run you to ground and even what I saw as the score between us—'

Predictably, Darcy cut to the heart of the matter. 'You thought I'd made a fool of you.'

'Yes…and that was a new experience for me. I must confess that there was nothing I was not prepared to do to achieve my objective,' Luca admitted with a grim edge to his dark, deep voice. 'If Ilaria hadn't confessed tonight, I'd still have believed you guilty, and since it would not have been possible for you to satisfy my demand that you help me to regain the Adorata…I would, ultimately, have dispossessed you of Fielding's Folly.'

Darcy was ashen pale now. 'No…you wouldn't have done that.'

Slowly, Luca shook his dark head, stunning dark eyes resting full on her disbelieving face. 'Darcy, you're a much nicer person than I have ever been…I *would* have done it. When I married you, I already held the future of the Folly in the palm of my hand.'

'What do you m-mean?' she stammered, moisture beading her short upper lip as she stared back at him.

From the inside pocket of his beautifully tailored dinner jacket, Luca withdrew a folded document. 'I bought the company which gave your father the mortgage on the Folly. This is the agreement. You're in default of the terms of that agreement now. I could have called in the loan and forced you out at any time over the next six months,' he spelt out very quietly. 'It would've been as easy as taking candy from a baby.'

Her shattered eyes huge dark smudges against her pallor, Darcy gazed back at him transfixed. 'You...you *bought* the company?' she gasped sickly.

As he absorbed the full extent of her horror at such calculated foreplanning, Luca seemed to pale too. 'I had to tell you. I had to be completely honest with you. You have the right to know it all now.'

Her lips bloodless, Darcy mumbled strickenly, 'I don't think I wanted to know that...how could anybody sink *that* low?'

'I wish I could say that I don't know what got into me...but I *do* know,' Luca murmured with bleak, dark eyes. 'My ego could not live with what I believed you had done to me that night. I had the power to take a terrible revenge and that was my intention when I replied to your advertisement.'

Darcy nodded like a little wooden marionette, too appalled to do anything but gaze back at him as if he had turned into a monster before her very eyes.

A faint sheen now glossed Luca's golden skin. 'Not a very pretty objective...when I think back to that now, I am very much ashamed. You have made such a valiant struggle to survive against all the odds.'

Darcy shook her pounding head with a little jerk. She felt as if she was dying inside, and now she knew what was really the matter with her—could no longer avoid knowing. She had fallen in love with him. How else could he be hurting her so much? She turned almost clumsily away from him, a mess of raw, agonised nerve-endings, and sank down onto a sofa. 'I *slept* with you,' she muttered, suddenly stricken.

'I definitely don't think we should touch on that issue right now,' Luca contended without hesitation. 'I'm sinking faster than a rock in a swamp as it is. What I want to do now...what I *need* to do...is make amends to you in every way possible.'

'I hate you...' And she did. She hated him because he didn't love her, because he had made a fool of her, because she had made a fool of herself and, last but not least, because she could not bear the thought of having to struggle to get over him again.

'I can live with that.'

'I want to go home.'

'Of course. The jet is at your disposal. When were you thinking of leaving?'

'Now—'

'It wouldn't be a good idea to get Zia out of bed.' Since Darcy was still staring numbly at the rug beneath her feet, Luca hunkered down in front of her. 'Shout at me...hit me if it makes you feel better. I don't know what to do when you're quiet!' he murmured fiercely.

'I'll leave first thing in the morning,' Darcy swore.

Luca reached for her tightly coiled hands. 'When do you want me to fly over?'

Darcy focused on him for the first time in several minutes but said nothing, her incredulity unfeigned.

Brilliant dark eyes glittered. 'You're stuck with me for the next six months,' Luca reminded her gently. 'Surely you hadn't forgotten that...had you?'

Darcy *had*. Her brain felt as if it was spinning in tortured circles.

Luca contrived to ease up each small coiled finger during the interim, and gain a hold on both of her hands. 'I promise to fulfil our agreement. No matter what happens, I will not let you down.'

Darcy snatched her hands back in a raw motion of repudiation. 'I couldn't *stand* it!'

'I have tried to express my remorse—'

'I don't think you have it in you to *feel* remorse!' Darcy condemned abruptly, her oval face flushing with a return

of healthier colour as she got her teeth into that conviction.
'You're sneaky, devious…and I can't abide sneakiness or
dishonesty. The only two things in life that excite you are
sex and money.'

A dark rise of blood had delineated the savagely taut
slant of his cheekbones. 'Once there was a third thing that
excited me, far more than either of those.'

'*What?*' she gibed with a jagged laugh as she sprang
upright, no longer able to stand being so close to him, terrified her fevered emotions would betray her. 'The prospect
of taking revenge? Gosh, I should be flattered! Was that
stupid bloody ring really worth this much effort?'

Luca vaulted back to his full commanding height, but
with something less than his habitual grace. 'No…' It was
very quiet.

'And do you want the biggest laugh of all?' Darcy slung
shakily at him, green eyes huge with pain, her slender body
trembling with the force of her feelings. 'I fell like a ton
of bricks for you that night, only I didn't realise until it
was too late. I even tried to find my way back to your
apartment but I couldn't! What a lucky miss! You'd have
had me arrested for theft before I'd cleared the front door!'

Luca looked poleaxed, as well he might have done.
Darcy hadn't meant to spill out such a private painful truth,
but she flung her head back with defiant pride, meeting the
sheer shock in his spectacular dark eyes without flinching.

'You went to the Ponte della Guerra,' he breathed with
ragged abruptness, catching her by surprise. 'No…please
tell me you *didn't!*'

'While you were ferreting like a great stupid prat round
your empty safe!' Taking a bold stance, Darcy stalked to
the door. 'Don't you dare show your face at the Folly for
a few weeks!'

'As we are supposed to be a newly married couple that
might arouse suspicion,' Luca pointed out flatly.

'Luca…you're not seeing the whole picture here!' Darcy
informed him with vigour. 'A honeymoon that lasts less

than three days has obviously been a wash-out! An absentee workaholic husband completes the right image for a marriage destined to fail. And when you do come to visit, and everyone sees how absolutely useless you are at being my strong right arm, nobody's going to be one bit surprised when I dump you six months down the line!'

# CHAPTER TEN

DARCY closed the glossy magazine with a barely restrained shudder, undyingly grateful that Luca would never read the interview she had given. At her request, the magazine had faxed the questions to her. After carefully studying some old magazines to see how other women had talked in similar interviews, Darcy had responded to those questions with a cringe-making amount of slush and gush.

Anyway, Luca was in Italy, and men *didn't* read those sort of publications, did they? The sizeable cheque she had earned for that tissue of lies about her blissfully happy marriage and her even more wonderful new husband was more than sufficient compensation for a little embarrassment. With the proceeds she would be able to bring the mortgage repayments up to date, settle some other outstanding bills and put the Land Rover in for a service.

It had been two weeks and three days since she had seen Luca. Every day, every hour had crawled. She felt *haunted* by Luca. Having him around to shout at or even ignore would have been infinitely more bearable. She ached for him. And she was angry and ashamed that she could feel such an overpowering need and hunger for a male who had entered her life only to harm her.

Impervious to all hints, and beautifully well-mannered to the last, Luca had seen them off at the airport. Zia had actually burst into tears when she realised that he wasn't coming with them. Lifting the little girl for a farewell hug, Luca had looked strangely self-satisfied. But seeing those two dark heads so close together had had a very different effect on Darcy.

The physical resemblance between father and daughter

was startling. The Raffacani straight nose and level brows, the black hair and dark eyes...Darcy was now confronting unwelcome realities. Zia had the right to know her father. And Luca had rights too—not that she thought he would have the slightest urge to exercise them.

But if she didn't tell Luca that he had a daughter, some day Zia would demand that her mother justify that decision. And the unhappy truth was that her own wounded pride, her craven desire to avoid a traumatic confession and her pessimistic suppositions about how Luca might react, were not in themselves sufficient excuse for her to remain silent.

Richard had phoned in the week to say that he would come down for a night over the weekend with his current girl-friend. Darcy had been looking forward to some fresh company, but unfortunately Richard arrived on Friday afternoon, just as she was on her way out with Zia. He was alone.

Tall, loose-limbed, and with a shock of dark hair and brown eyes, Richard immediately made himself at home on the sagging sofa by the kitchen range. 'If you're going out, I intend to drown my sorrows,' he warned, his mobile features radiating self-pity in waves. 'I've been dumped.'

Darcy almost said, Not *again,* which would have been very tactless. Managing to bite the words back, she gave his slumped shoulder a consoling pat. He was like the brother she had never had, and utterly clueless about women. He had a fatal weakness for long-legged glamorous blondes, and the looks and the money to attract them if not to hold them. He didn't like clubbing or parties. He lived for his horses. He was a man with a Porsche in search of a rare, horsy homebody hiding behind the façade of a long-legged glamorous blonde.

'Zia's been invited to a party and I offered to stay and help,' Darcy told him. 'I'll be a while, so you're on your own unless you care to ring Karen.'

'Pity *she's* not a blonde,' Richard lamented, stuck like a

record in a groove. He pulled a whisky bottle out of a capacious pocket. 'None of the women I like are blonde…'

'Doesn't that tell you something?'

'I wish I'd done the decent thing and married you. I probably would've been quite happy.'

'Richard…' Darcy drew in a deep, restraining breath, reminded that she had yet to tell Richard that she was currently in possession of a husband. 'Why don't you put the booze away and go down to the lodge and keep Karen company?'

'I'm not telling *her* I've been dumped again…she'd *laugh!*'

Darcy called Karen before she went out. 'Richard's here,' she announced. 'He's been dumped.'

Karen howled with laughter.

'I thought I'd let you get that out of your system before you see him in the flesh.'

It was almost seven by the time Darcy arrived home. After all the excitement at the party, Zia was exhausted and ready only for bed. Richard was in a maudlin slump in the kitchen. Darcy surveyed the sunken level on the whisky bottle in dismay. 'You're feeling *that* bad?'

'Worsh,' Richard groaned, opening only one bloodshot eye.

Pity and irritation mingled inside Darcy. She, too, was miserable. Some decent conversation might have cheered her up, but Richard was drunk as a skunk. And, since he had never behaved like that before, she couldn't even reasonably shout at him.

She took Zia upstairs, gave her a quick bath, tucked her into bed and started to read her a story, but Zia fell asleep in the middle of it. Her eyes filled with guilt and love, Darcy smoothed her daughter's dark curls tenderly from her brow and sighed. She owed it to Zia to tell Luca the truth.

With a steely glint in her gaze, Darcy went back downstairs to sort out Richard. Since he'd chosen to get legless in her absence, he could jolly well go and sleep it off.

'Time for bed, Richard,' she announced loudly. 'Get up!'

He lumbered upright in slow and very shaky motion. 'Ish still light...' he muttered in bewilderment.

'*So?*' Darcy pushed him towards the stairs. 'You're lucky Karen's not here...you know how she feels about alcohol after her experiences with her ex.'

Richard looked terrified. 'Not coming, ish she?'

Reflecting on the awkwardness of having two close friends who occasionally mixed like oil and water, she guided him into the room beside her own, which she had once promised Luca. Richard lurched down onto the mattress like a falling tree.

'Met your hushband...when did you get a hushband?' Richard contrived to slur, with only academic interest.

In the act of throwing a blanket over his prone body Darcy stilled, not crediting what she was hearing. 'My husband?' she queried sharply.

Grabbing her hand, Richard tugged her closer and whispered confidentially, '*Not* a friendly chap...tried to hit me...would've punched my lights out if I hadn't fallen over...'

He was rambling, out of his skull, hallucinating. He *had* to be.

'Now isn't this cosy?' A dark sardonic drawl breathed at that exact same moment from the doorway.

Darcy got such a shock she almost leapt a foot in the air. An incredulous look on her face, she wrenched herself free of Richard and whipped round. 'Where did you come from?' she gasped, totally appalled and showing it. 'I've been home over an hour!'

'Since you were out, I went for a drive,' Luca divulged grimly.

And she looked awful, she reflected in anguish. Before bathing Zia she had sensibly changed into a faded summer dress. Had she known Luca was coming, she would have dressed up—*not* because she wished to attract him, but because she didn't want him thinking, Gosh, what a mess she is. What did I ever see in her? She had her pride and now it was in the dust.

Luca, clad in yet another of his breathtakingly elegant suits, looked absolutely stupendous. Navy suit, white shirt with fine red stripes, red silk tie. Smart enough to stroll out in front of television cameras. Slowly, very slowly, she allowed her intimidated gaze to rise above his shirt collar. Jawline aggressive. Beautiful mouth grim. Spectacular cheekbones harshly prominent and flushed. Sensational eyes blazing like gold daggers locking into a target.

Her mouth ran dry, her heart skipping a beat.

The very image of masculine outrage, Luca continued to stare at her, the sheer force of his will beating down on her. 'Carlton is *not* staying the night here!'

Richard opened his eyes. 'Thash him,' he said helpfully. 'Speaksh Italian like a native...'

'Oh, do shut up and go to sleep, Richard,' Darcy muttered unevenly.

'He stays...*I go*,' Luca delivered in a charged undertone.

'Don't be daft...he's not doing you any harm!'

Luca spun on his heel. Darcy unfroze and flew through the door after him. 'Luca...where are you going?'

He shot her a scorching look of incredulous fury. 'I'm leaving. *Per amor di Dio*... I will not stay beneath the same roof as your lover!'

'Are you out of your mind?' Darcy demanded, wide-eyed. 'Richard is *not* my lover.'

His shimmering eyes murderous, Luca spread both hands in a slashing motion and shot something at her in wrathful Italian.

Darcy gulped, registering that she was dealing with a seethingly angry male, presently incapable of accepting reasoned argument or explanation and indeed at the very limit of his control. 'OK...OK, I'll get rid of him,' she promised in desperation, because she knew at that moment that if she didn't, it was the end of everything. Luca would depart never to return.

She lifted the phone by the bed and dialled the lodge. 'Karen…I need a very big favour from you…in fact, it's so big I don't quite know how to ask. Richard is drunk, Luca's here and he's got this ridiculous idea that Richard and I are lovers. He's really furious and he wants him out of the house, and I—'

'Richard, drunk…?' Karen interrupted that frantic flood. 'Helpless, is he?'

'Pretty much. Could you possibly give him a bed for the night?' Darcy felt awful making such a request.

'Oh, yes…' Karen coughed suddenly, evidently clearing her throat, and added very stiffly, 'Yes, I suppose I could.'

'Thanks.' Darcy sagged with relief.

'We're going to go for a little walk, Richard,' she said winsomely as she yanked the blanket off him again.

Running through his pockets, she extracted his car keys and, anchoring a long arm round her shoulder, tried to haul him off the bed. 'Richard…you weigh a ton!' she groaned in frustration.

'Allow me,' Luca breathed savagely from behind her.

In dismay, Darcy released her hold on Richard. In a display of far from reassuring strength, Luca accomplished the feat of getting Richard upright again.

'Where are you taking him?' Luca demanded roughly.

'Not far. Just get him down into his car. Don't…don't hurt him,' she muttered anxiously on the stairs, as Richard staggered and Luca anchored a hand as gentle as a meat hook into the back of his sweater.

Richard loaded up, Darcy swung into the driver's seat of the Porsche and ignited the engine.

'Where we goin'?' Richard mumbled.

'You'll see.' She didn't have the heart to tell him. He had found himself at the withering end of Karen's sharp and clever tongue too often. Handing him over drunk and incapable of self-defence was the equivalent of handing a baby to a cannibal.

Karen had heard the car. She walked out into the lane

and had the passenger door open before Darcy had even alighted.

'*Karen…?*' Richard was moaning in horror.

'Relax, Richard,' Karen purred, sounding all maternal and caring. 'I'm going to look after you.'

Darcy gaped at her friend over the car bonnet. 'Karen…what's going on?'

'Have you any idea how long I've waited for a chance like this?' Karen whispered back, her eyes gleaming as she reached up to smooth a soothing hand over Richard's tousled dark hair. 'Blondes are bad news for you, Richard,' she told him in a mesmeric tone of immense compassion.

'Yesh,' Darcy heard Richard agree slavishly as Karen guided him slowly towards the lodge.

Karen was either planning to lull Richard into a false sense of security before she turned a hose on him in the back garden to sober him up, or she was planning to persuade Richard that his dream woman had finally arrived in the unexpected shape of a small but very attractive brunette.

Darcy walked back up to the Folly. Luca was waiting in the hall for her. He didn't even stop to draw breath. 'What was that drunken idiot doing here tonight?' he demanded rawly.

'For goodness' sake, he often stays, and he doesn't normally drink like that. He brings his girlfriends here too,' Darcy proffered tautly. 'I don't know where you get the idea that we're lovers—'

'Three years ago, you almost married Carlton. *He jilted you!*' Luca reminded her savagely. '*Porca miseria*…do you expect me to believe that he's now only a platonic friend?'

'Yes, I do expect you to believe that.' Darcy met his burnished gaze levelly.

'Even though he's the father of your child?' Luca framed with driven ferocity.

Darcy turned pale as milk. 'I assure you that Zia is *not* Richard's child.'

The tense silence simmered, but she saw some of the tension ease in Luca's angry stance.

Desperate to know what Luca was thinking now that she had made that admission, Darcy murmured tautly, 'Until Richard and I both fell for other people, neither of us realised what was missing in our relationship. We stayed friends. He's a terrific guy, kind, caring…'

Luca's mouth twisted as he listened, hooded eyes hard as stones as he followed her into the drawing room. 'Mr Wonderful…Mr Perfect…'

'No…he does tend to tell the same horsy stories and jokes over and over again.'

Darcy was surprised that he had made no further comment on the subject of Zia's paternity. Heavens, did he still think there had been other men in her life, then?

'And he's thicker than a block of wood…don't forget that minor imperfection,' Luca slotted in drily. 'But why didn't you tell him that you're married? *Accidenti*…so close a friend and he didn't even know I existed!'

'Tonight was the first time I'd seen him since our wedding, but I didn't have time to talk to him because I had to go out. When did you arrive?'

'After six. I did not expect to arrive here and find another man in residence!'

Darcy blinked, and thought about the last enervating half-hour. Luca had behaved like a jealous, possessive husband and instinctively she had reacted like a foolish and insecure new wife, eager to placate him. Luca, jealous? It was a stunning concept.

'Were you jealous when you thought Richard was my lover?' Darcy asked baldly.

Luca stilled and sent her a gleaming glance from below inky black lashes. 'I am naturally jealous of my dignity.'

'Your dignity?' Her hopeful face had fallen by a mile.

'Is it unreasonable for me to expect you to behave like a normal wife?' Luca countered levelly. 'In the light of your previous relationship with him, inviting Carlton to stay here alone with you was most unwise—'

'Unwise,' Darcy parroted, thinking what a bloodless, passionless word that was.

'As my wife, you are now in the public eye, and a potential target for damaging gossip. Surely you can't want anyone to have cause to suspect at this early stage that there is anything seriously wrong with our marriage?'

Darcy slowly nodded. He wasn't jealous. He was just an arrogant, macho male, determined to preserve his own public image. People might laugh if they suspected his wife was being unfaithful, and he wouldn't like that.

'By the way, I settled your mortgage,' Luca remarked with stupendous casualness.

Darcy's lower lip parted company with her upper in shock.

Brilliant dark eyes intent on her aghast expression, Luca continued smoothly, 'As you're so independent, I imagine you'll wish to repay me once you inherit your godmother's money, but in the short term you are no longer burdened by those substantial monthly payments.'

Darcy stumbled into speech. 'But, Luca…what right—?'

'I haven't finished yet. I have also had a word with your bank manager. There is no longer a limit on your overdraft. Don't throw it all back in my face,' he urged almost roughly, openly assessing her shaken, troubled face. 'I had no *right* to interfere, but I had a very powerful *need* to offer you what help I could.'

Still reeling, Darcy swallowed hard. She understood, oh, yes, she understood. Luca felt guilty. This was his way of making amends. His intervention on such grounds filled her with pained discomfiture, but she was in no position to refuse his efforts on behalf of the estate. He was making it possible for her to survive and re-employ the staff.

'Thanks,' she said stiltedly.

'I would have liked to do a great deal more, *cara mia,*'

Luca admitted steadily. 'But I knew you wouldn't have accepted that.'

At that respectful acknowledgement, a slow, uncertain smile drove the tension from her tense mouth. 'Did you park your wings outside?'

'My wings?'

'You'd make a really good guardian angel.'

'I was afraid you were about to say fairy godmother,' Luca confided.

'It did cross my mind.' Darcy wrinkled her nose and laughed for the first time in weeks. And then she remembered what she still had to tell him and her face shadowed. Tomorrow, she decided, she would tell him tomorrow…

It was half past eight when the Victorian bell on the massive front door shrieked and jangled.

Luca was in the library, having excused himself to make some calls, and Darcy had gone upstairs to slide into an outfit that magically accentuated her every slender curve. Green, with a fashionably short skirt and fitted jacket. She thought it looked kind of sexy on her. She slid her feet into high heels and fiddled anxiously with her hair in the mirror. And the whole time she was engaged on that transformation she refused to think about *why* she was doing it.

When Darcy opened the door, out of breath from rushing full tilt down the stairs, her sensitive stomach somersaulted when she saw Margo and Nina standing outside. Her stepmother elegant in black, and her stepsister dressed to kill in a sugar-pink dress so perilously short it made Darcy's skirt look like a maxi.

Both women did a rather exaggerated double take over her altered image.

'Is that a Galliano?' Nina demanded in an envious shriek.

'A…a what?' Darcy countered blankly.

'And those shoes are Prada! He got you out of your Barbour and your wellies fast enough!' Nina gibed thinly.

'It's such a dangerous sign when a man tries to change a woman into something she's not.'

On her lofty passage towards the drawing room, Margo winced. 'And green simply *screams* at your red hair, Darcy!'

'But Darcy doesn't have *red* hair,' a deep, dark drawl interceded across the depth of the hall from the library doorway. 'It's Titian, a shade defined by the dictionary as a bright, golden auburn.'

Darcy threw Luca the sort of look a drowning swimmer gives to a life jacket.

Margo and Nina weren't quite quick enough to conceal their dismay and surprise at Luca's appearance.

'I understood that you were still in Italy, Luca.' Her step-mother's smile of greeting was stiff.

'I thought that might be why you were here.' As Luca strolled over to the fireplace and took up a relaxed stance there, he let that statement hang a split-second, while their uninvited visitors tensed with uncertainty at his possible meaning before continuing smoothly, 'How very kind of you to think that Darcy might be in need of company.'

'I'm sure Richard Carlton's been dropping in too,' Nina said innocently.

'Yes, and what a very entertaining guy he is,' Luca countered, smiling without skipping a beat while Darcy's fascinated gaze darted back and forth between the combatants. Margo and Nina had definitely met their match.

'Nina and I were only saying yesterday what a coincidence it is that Darcy and Maxie Kendall should have got married within weeks of each other!' Margo exclaimed, watching Darcy stiffen with suspicious eyes. 'Now what was the name of Nancy Leeward's other godchild?'

'Polly,' Darcy muttered tightly. 'Why?'

'Naturally I'm curious. That old woman left such an extraordinary will! I expect we'll be hearing of Polly's marriage next...'

'I doubt it,' Darcy slotted in. 'When I last saw her, Polly had no plans to marry.'

Nina directed a brilliant smile at Luca and crossed her fabulous long legs, her abbreviated dress riding so high Darcy wouldn't have been surprised to see pantie elastic. 'I bet you haven't a clue what we're talking about, Luca.'

Margo chimed in, 'I'm afraid it did cross my mind that Darcy might—'

'Might marry me to inherit a measly one million?' Sardonic amusement gleamed in Luca's steady appraisal. 'Yes, of course I know about the will, but I can assure you that an eccentric godmother's wishes played no part whatsoever in *my* desire to marry your stepdaughter.'

'Yes,' Darcy agreed, getting into the spirit of his game with dancing green eyes. 'I believe Luca would say that when he married me, he had his own private agenda.'

'*Ouch,*' Luca breathed for her ears alone, and her cheeks warmed.

But Margo was not so easily silenced. 'I don't know how to put this without seeming intrusive…but frankly I was concerned when I learnt from friends locally that Darcy had come home alone after spending only forty-eight hours with you in Venice—'

'Mummy…it's hardly likely to be her favourite place,' Nina said with a meaningful look.

'I love Venice,' Darcy returned squarely.

'I know you gave your poor child that silly name—Venezia—but I notice you soon gave up using it,' Margo reminded her drily.

'*Venezia?*' Luca queried abruptly.

Darcy's sensitive insides turned a sick somersault. She encountered a narrowed stare of bemusement from Luca and turned her head away abruptly.

'Such a silly name!' Nina giggled. 'But then Darcy never did have much taste or discretion.'

Darcy felt too sick to glance again in Luca's direction.

Her nerves were shot to hell. She wanted to put a sack over Nina and suffocate her before she said too much.

'Your sense of humour must often cause deep offence,' Luca drawled with chilling bite, studying Nina with contempt. 'I have zero tolerance for anything that might distress my wife.'

Two rosy high spots of red embellished Nina's cheeks. Heavens, Darcy thought in equal shock, he sounded so incredibly protective. Her strain eased as she realised that Nina had abandoned her intent to make further snide comments about Zia.

'Yes, you were very thoughtless, Nina,' Margo agreed sharply. 'That's all in the past now. I actually came here today to express my very genuine concern over something Darcy has done.'

'Really, Margo?' Darcy was emboldened by the supportive hand Luca had settled in the shallow indentation of her spine.

'You brought Luca to the engagement party I held and not one word did you breathe about his exalted status,' Margo returned thinly.

Too enervated to be able to guess what her stepmother was leading up to, Darcy saw no relevance whatsoever to that statement.

'So what on earth persuaded you to do *this?*' Her stepmother drew a folded magazine from her capacious bag, her face stiff with distaste and disapproval. 'Is there *anything* you wouldn't do for money, Darcy? How could you embarrass your husband like that?'

Instant appalled paralysis afflicted Darcy. Her green eyes zoomed in on the magazine which contained that dreadful gushing interview, and in the same second she turned the colour of a ripe tomato, her stomach curdling with horror. Embarrassment choked her.

Margo shook her blonde head pityingly. 'I was horrified that Darcy should sell the story of your marriage to a lurid gossip magazine, Luca.'

'Whereas I shall treasure certain phrases spoken in that interview for ever,' Luca purred in a tone of rich complacency, extending his arm to ease Darcy's trembling, anxious length into the hard, muscular heat of his big frame. 'When I read about Darcy's "mystical sense of wonder" and her "spiritual feeling of soul-deep recognition" on first meeting me, I envied her ability to verbalise sensations and sentiments which I myself could never find adequate words to describe.'

'Luca?' Darcy mumbled shakily, shattered that he had actually read that interview and absorbed sufficient of her mindless drivel to quote directly from it.

But Luca, it seemed, was in full appreciative flow. 'Indeed, I was overwhelmed by such a powerful need to be with Darcy again I flew straight here to her side. I shall *always* regard that interview as an open love letter from my wife.'

For the space of ten seconds Margo and Nina just sat there, apparently transfixed.

'Of course, I'm very relieved to hear that the interview hasn't caused any friction between you. I was *so* worried it would,' Margo responded unconvincingly.

'You surprise me.' Fabulous bone structure grim, eyes wintry, Luca studied their visitors. 'Only a fool could fail to see through your foolish attempts to diminish Darcy in my eyes. She is a woman of integrity, and how she contrived to hang onto that integrity growing up with two such vicious women is nothing short of a miracle!'

'How dare you talk to me like that?' Margo gasped, rising to her feet in sheer shock.

'You resent my wife's ownership of an estate which has been within her family for over four hundred years. You're furious that she has married a rich man who will help her to retain that home. You hoped she would be forced to sell up because you planned to demand a share of the proceeds,' Luca condemned with sizzling distaste. 'That is why I dare to talk to you as I have.'

'I'm not staying here to be insulted,' Margo snapped, stalking towards the door.

'I think that's very wise.'

Luca listened to the thud of the massive front door with complete calm.

Stunned at what had just transpired, Darcy breathed. 'I need to check on Zia…'

'Venezia,' Luca murmured softly, catching her taut fingers in his as she started up the stairs. 'Obviously you chose that name because it held a special significance for you. You were happy with me that night in Venice?'

'Y-yes,' Darcy stammered.

'But we met in what was clearly a troubled and transitional phase of your life.' His lean, strong features were taut, as if he was selecting his words with great care. 'I understand now why you so freely forgave Carlton for jilting you. Evidently he wasn't the only guilty party. You went to bed with someone other than him before that wedding.'

'No, I didn't!' Angry chagrined colour warmed Darcy's face as she stopped dead in the corridor.

'*Accidenti!* What's the point of denying it?' Luca demanded in exasperation. 'You may well not have been aware of the fact that night, but you *were* pregnant when you first met me!'

'No…I wasn't,' Darcy told him staunchly, pressing open the door of Zia's bedroom. 'You're still barking up the wrong tree!'

'You must've been pregnant,' Luca contradicted steadily, as if he was dealing with a child fearfully reluctant to own up to misbehaviour. 'Your daughter was born seven months later.'

'Zia was premature. She spent weeks in hospital before I could bring her home…' Darcy held her breath in the silence which followed, and then steeled herself to turn and face him.

Luca had a dazed, disconcerted look in his dark, deep-set eyes. He stared at her. 'She was premature?' he breathed, so low he had to clear his throat to be audible.

'So you see, now that you've been through the butcher, the baker and the candlestick-maker, as they say in the nursery rhyme, we're running out of possible culprits,' Darcy pointed out unsteadily, her throat tight, her mouth dry, her heart thumping like mad behind her breastbone. 'And to be honest, there only ever *was* one possibility, Luca.'

In the dim light, his eyes suddenly flashed pure gold. 'Are you trying to tell me that...that Zia is mine?' he whispered raggedly.

# CHAPTER ELEVEN

DARCY'S voice let her down when she most needed it. As Luca asked that loaded question she gave a fierce, jerky nod, and she didn't take her strained gaze from him for a second.

Black spiky lashes screened his sensational eyes. He blinked. He was stunned.

Darcy swallowed and relocated her voice. 'And there's not any doubt about it because Richard and I never slept together. We had decided to wait until we were married.'

'*Never?*' Luca stressed with hoarse incredulity.

Darcy grimaced. 'And, since we didn't *get* married, we never actually made it to bed.'

'That means…but that means that I would've been your first…*impossible—!*' Luca broke off and compressed his lips, studying her with shaken dark eyes.

Darcy reddened. 'I didn't want you to guess that night. You said virgins were deeply unexciting,' she reminded him accusingly.

'We both said and did several foolish things that night…but fortunately making Zia was not one of them.' With a roughened laugh that betrayed the emotions he was struggling to contain, Luca closed his hands on hers to draw her closer while he gazed endlessly down at Zia, and then back at Darcy, as if he was being torn in two different directions. '*Per amor di Dio*…the truth has been staring me in the face from the start,' he groaned. 'The fact that nobody knew who the father of your child was. You wouldn't say because you *couldn't* say…you didn't even know my name!'

Her anxious eyes were vulnerably wide.

173

Slowly Luca shook his glossy dark head. 'I saw that photo of Carlton, and he's dark as well. I assumed he was her father and that you still loved him enough to protect him. Then, when you said he wasn't, it *still* didn't occur to me that she could be my child!'

'You didn't know Zia was born prematurely. She arrived more than six weeks early.'

'I want to wake her up to look at her properly,' Luca confided a little breathlessly as he suddenly released Darcy to look down at his daughter. 'But that's the first lesson she taught me. Don't disturb her when she's asleep!'

'She sleeps like the dead, Luca.'

'Where were my *eyes?*' he whispered in unconcealed wonder. 'She has my nose—'

'She got just about everything from you.' As she hovered there Darcy was feeling slightly abandoned, and, pessimist that she had been, she was unprepared for Luca's obvious excitement at the discovery that he was a father.

Excitement? No, she certainly hadn't expected that. But then nothing had gone remotely like any of her vague imaginings of this scene. Luca had been shocked, but he had skipped the mortifying protest stage she had feared and gone straight into acceptance mode.

'She's really beautiful,' Luca commented with considerable pride.

'Yes, I think so too,' Darcy whispered rather forlornly.

'*Per meraviglia*…I'm a father. I'd better get on to my lawyer straight away—'

'I beg your pardon? Your lawyer?'

'If I was to drop dead tonight before I acknowledge her as my daughter, she could end up penniless!' Luca headed straight for the door. 'I'll call him right now.'

*Drop dead, then, Luca.* Darcy's eyes prickled and stung. She sniffed. Of course she didn't mean that. In fact just thinking of anything happening to Luca pierced her to the heart and terrified her, but it was hard to cope with feeling like the invisible woman.

'Aren't you coming?' Luca glanced back in at her again.

She sat in the library, watching him call his lawyer. Then he called his sister, and by the sound of the squeals of excitement Ilaria was delighted to receive such a stunning announcement.

'Zia is mine. Obviously it was meant to be,' Luca drawled, squaring his shoulders as he sank down into the armchair opposite her. 'Now I want to hear everything from the first minute you suspected you might be pregnant.'

'I was about five months gone before I worked that out.'

'Five *months?*' Luca exclaimed.

'I didn't put on much weight, didn't have any morning sickness or anything. I *was* eating a lot, and I got a bit of a tummy, and then I got this *really* weird sort of little fluttery feeling…that's what made me go to the doctor. When he told me it was the baby moving I was shocked rigid!'

'I imagine you were.' Luca's spectacular dark eyes were brimming with tender amusement. Rising lithely from his chair, he settled down on the sofa beside her and reached for her hand to close it between his long fingers. 'So you weren't ill?'

'Healthy as a horse.'

'And how did your family react?'

'My father was pretty decent about it, but I think that was because he was hoping I'd have a boy,' Darcy admitted ruefully. 'He didn't give two hoots about the gossip, but Margo was ready to kill me. She went round letting everyone believe the baby was Richard's because, of course, that sounded rather better.'

'What did you tell your family about Zia's father?'

'More or less the truth…ships that pass…said I'd *forgotten* your name,' Darcy admitted shamefacedly.

'How alone you must have felt,' Luca murmured heavily, his grip on her small hand tightening. 'But that night you gave me to understand that you were protected.'

'I honestly thought I was. I didn't realise that you had to take those wretched contraceptive pills continuously to be safe...and, of course, I'd tossed them in the bin the first morning I was in Venice!'

'If *only* you hadn't run away from the apartment—'

'You'd have stuck the police on me instead.'

'I wouldn't have. Had you stayed, your innocence would never have been in doubt. *Why?*' Luca emphasised, intent, dark golden eyes holding her more evasive gaze. 'Why did you run away?'

'It's pretty embarrassing waking up for the first time in a strange man's bed,' Darcy said bluntly. 'I felt like a real tart—'

'You don't know the first thing about being a tart, so don't use that word,' Luca censured with frowning reproof.

But a split second later he was smiling that utterly charismatic smile of his, sending her heartbeat bumpety-bumpety-bump as he asked all sorts of questions about Zia, demonstrating a degree of interest that was encyclopaedic in its detail. At the end of that session, he murmured with considerable assurance, 'Well...there'll be no divorce now, *cara mia.*'

Even though that development was what Darcy had hoped for from the instant she knew that she loved Luca, she didn't like the background against which he had formed that instant arrogant supposition. She tugged her hand free of his, her face frozen. 'Why? Do you know something I don't?'

Luca dealt her a startled, questioning look. 'We have a child. She needs both of us. I simply assumed—'

'I don't think you should be assuming anything in that line!' Darcy told him roundly. 'It may be important that Zia has a father, but I'm concerned about what *I* need too.'

'You need me,' Luca breathed a shade harshly, all relaxation now wiped from his taut features and not a hint of a smile left either.

Darcy flew upright. 'Don't look at me like that!'

'In what way am I looking at you?' Luca enquired forbiddingly.

'Like I'm a bad debtor or something, and you're…you're trying to work out my Achilles' heel!' Suddenly frightened by the awareness that she was heading for an argument with him and that she didn't want that, didn't trust her own over-wrought and confused emotions, or her too often danger-ously blunt tongue, she said tightly, 'Look, I'm very tired. I'm going up to bed.'

From the foot of the stairs she glanced back into the library. Luca was standing by the window, ferocious ten-sion screaming from his stillness. Her heart sank at the sight. Everything had gone wrong from the moment she questioned his conviction that they should now view their marriage as a real marriage. And why the heck had she done that? Why, when she herself longed for that stupid agreement they had made to be set aside and totally wiped from both their memories? Why had she refused the offer of her own most heartfelt wish?

And she saw into herself then, was forced to confront her own insecurity. She feared that Luca only wanted their marriage to continue for Zia's benefit. Hadn't she felt threatened and excluded by his unashamed absorption and delight in Zia? How foolish and selfish that had been, on the very night he first learned that he was a father!

Feeling considerably less bolshie, Darcy made up her bed with fresh sheets. She took the dogs down the service stairs to sleep in the kitchen. Then she donned a strappy oyster-coloured satin nightie and slid between the sheets to wait for Luca.

But an hour later, when she heard footsteps in the cor-ridor and tensed with a fast-beating heart, Luca passed by her room. In the silence of the old house she listened to him enter the room Richard had briefly occupied earlier and close the door.

She fell back against the pillows then, shaken, hurt and scared…utterly out of her depth with this Luca who was not even tempted to make love to her after an absence of three weeks.

\*      \*      \*

'Fabulous apartment,' Karen sighed when she arrived for lunch, scanning the fantastic view of London from the penthouse. 'And Luca…he is *the* perfect man; I am totally convinced of that. The guy that clears off without a murmur so that you can have lunch with your best friend is special, and when he takes the toddler with him, he zooms up the scale of perfection and hits the bell at the top!'

'He's a very committed father.'

'I wouldn't say he was a slow starter in the husband stakes either. In one month, he has transformed your life. He even brings you flowers and cute little gifts… Richard's not into flowers, but he gave me a sweater covered with embroidered horseshoes for my birthday. It is the most *gross* garment you have ever seen, but he phones me about five times a day, and he's so scared I'm going to dump him, it's unbelievable,' Karen shared with a rather dreamy smile.

'I'm glad you're happy.'

'Well, you don't look glad enough to satisfy me,' Karen responded drily. 'I hope you're not turning into one of those spoilt little rich madams who can't appreciate what she's got!'

Darcy managed to laugh. 'Can you see the day?'

'No, but I know by your expression that there's something badly wrong, and that was an easy way to open the subject!'

Darcy thought back over the last four weeks. The Folly estate was now employing a full quota of staff, not to mention giving added employment to all the local firms engaged in the repairs and improvements which Luca had insisted the house required without further delay. While that work was going on they had set up temporary home in London at Luca's apartment, and when the summer was over they were shifting to Venice, where they would make their permanent home.

'Has he got another woman?'

'Of course he hasn't!' Darcy said, aghast.

'He's not violent or alcoholic or anything like that, is he?'

'*Karen!*' Darcy took a deep breath. 'He just doesn't love me.'

'*This* is the problem that has you moping about like a wet weekend?' Karen breathed incredulously. 'Luca arranges to fly me up here in a helicopter to have lunch with you as a surprise...he hangs on your every word, watches your every move...I mean, the guy's so besotted he's practically turning somersaults to impress!'

Darcy shrugged, unimpressed, gloom creeping over her again. They were sleeping in separate bedrooms. He hadn't made the slightest move to change that. It was as if sex didn't exist any more. And she couldn't forget that he had once admitted that possibly his belief that she was a thief had been the most dangerous part of her attraction. And it *was* as if her sex appeal had vanished overnight. Yet, aside from that, loads of really positive things were happening in their relationship...

Although she wasn't sure that being more hopelessly in love with Luca than ever was a positive thing. He was being caring, kind, supportive and considerate of her every need bar the one. He never lost his temper—no, not even when Zia had drawn all over a set of important business documents that had had to be replaced at supersonic speed before a big meeting. He took her out to dinner all the time. He took her to parties. He behaved as if he was very proud of her and paid her lots of compliments. He laughed, he smiled, he was a dirty great ray of constant sunshine, but when night fell he climbed into his *own* bed.

'Have you mentioned that you love *him* yet? I don't think it would be immediately obvious from your current demeanour,' Karen opined rather drily. 'Or maybe he's just not very good with the words.'

An hour after Karen's departure for home, Zia bounced into her mother's bedroom to show off the latest pair of new frilly socks on display. They had three layers of hand-made lace round the ankle. She was tickled pink with them. Zia was just one great big sunny smile these days. She had her mother, her adoring father and a devoted nanny, not to mention shelves groaning with toys. As she danced out again, a restive bundle of energy, Luca strolled in.

'Did you enjoy seeing Karen?' he enquired.

'Yes, it was great...I should've invited her up myself, but I knew she wouldn't want to be away for long, not with her romance with Richard hotting up the way it is.'

Just looking at him, she felt her mouth run dry and her pulses race. So she had learnt *not* to look at him directly. One quick, sneaky glance and then away again. If he didn't find her attractive any more, then the very last thing she needed was for him to guess that she was suffering withdrawal symptoms of the severest, cruellest kind. But that one sneaky glance she stole was enough to send her dizzy. Either Luca literally *did* get more gorgeous with every passing day, or she was more than usually susceptible.

In her mind's eye, she summoned him up. Casual silver-grey suit, superbly fitted to his wide shoulders, lithe hips and long powerful legs, worn with a cashmere sweater the colour of charcoal. He radiated sex appeal in waves she could *feel*. In much the same way that secret radar could feel the impact of those stunning dark eyes of his watching her.

'Darcy...I invited Karen here in the hope that you would relax with her,' Luca imparted tautly. 'But it doesn't seem to have done much good.'

'You can't put a plaster on something that isn't broken.'

'Is that one of those strange English nursery sayings?' Luca enquired.

Darcy didn't even know why she had said it, except to fill the tense silence, so she wasn't able to help him there. She twisted back to him but didn't meet his eyes.

'You know something, *cara mia?*' Luca breathed in a dangerous tone. 'I have decided that tact, patience and sensitivity do not work with you.'

'Probably not,' Darcy conceded, wondering why he had raised his voice slightly.

'In fact any man foolish enough to devote himself to the hopeless task of winning your trust would probably hit his deathbed before he got there.'

'Winning my trust?' Darcy repeated.

'What the hell do you think I've been doing for the past month?' Luca suddenly splintered at her in raw frustration.

And the strands of pain in that intonation made her look straight at him. She saw the same lonely ache there that she saw in her own face every time she stared in the mirror, and she stilled in shock.

Luca spread his hands in a familiar gesture that tugged at her heart. 'One minute you give me hope, the next you push me down,' he groaned. 'I don't need you to tell me that I made an appalling hash of our relationship, but I've been trying really hard to make up for that...only you seem to be getting further and further away from me, and I can't *bear* that when I love you so much!'

'You...you *love* me?' Darcy whispered shakily.

'You told me that you fell for me, too, that night in Venice, and that gave me hope.'

'If you love me why have you been sleeping in another room?' Darcy demanded accusingly. 'Why don't you touch me any more?'

Luca gave her a sincerely pained appraisal. 'I wanted you to appreciate that I *really* loved you.'

'Bloody funny way of showing it,' she mumbled helplessly, not knowing whether she was on her head or her heels. 'I've been so miserable.'

In one stride, Luca closed the distance between them. 'I was waiting for you to give me some sign that you still wanted me...I couldn't afford to take *anything* for granted about this marriage!'

'If you love me,' Darcy breathed headily, 'you can take me for granted all you like.'

With a muffled groan, Luca brought his mouth down

hard on hers and set off a devastating chain reaction of lust through her entire quivering body. He crushed her so close she couldn't breathe, backed up towards the door to turn the lock and then lifted his dark head again. 'I've never been so frustrated in my life...I *ache* for you, *cara mia*.'

She let her hand travel up over one blunt cheekbone in a caress and framed his face, her eyes full of love. 'Me too... I've been pretty stupid, putting my pride ahead of everything, closing you out when I needed you instead of showing it. I love you loads...and loads...and loads,' she told him a little tearfully, because her emotions were running so high they were right up there with the clouds. 'You should've been able to tell that a mile off!'

'You wouldn't even look at me any more!'

She gave him a flirtatious scrutiny from below curling lashes as he drew her hand down from his face and planted a kiss in the centre of her palm. 'You're a minx,' he told her huskily.

'I like the guy to do all the running. You see, the one time I did it the other way round, I ended up climbing out of a window with a burglar alarm screaming—and I also ended up pregnant,' she pointed out in her own defence.

'Zia's so precious, she could never be a source of regret,' Luca countered. 'I really fell for you in a very big way that night three years ago.'

'I find that so hard to believe—'

'That's because you don't think enough of yourself,' he scolded. 'You knocked me for six. You were so different from every other woman I had ever met. I fell asleep that night with you in my arms, and I felt pretty damned smug and self-satisfied—'

'And then it all went horribly wrong.'

'And I spent three insanely frustrating years trying to track you down... Make no mistake, I *was* totally obsessed,' Luca confided ruefully. 'I never admitted to myself how I really felt about you, but I could hardly wait for our neath that cool front.' Darcy gave a little feeling wriggle to stress how much she liked that.

'Has anybody ever told you how unbelievably sexy you look in wellington boots?'

She giggled, something she never did. 'I really, really believe that you love me now!'

Reaching up to claim his sensual mouth for herself again, Darcy gave herself up to the promise of a future full of blissful contentment and joy.

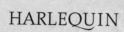

# My Secret Admirer

Savor the magic of love
with three new romances
from top-selling authors
**Anne Stuart,
Vicki Lewis Thompson and
Marisa Carroll.**

*My Secret Admirer* is a unique collection
of three brand-new stories featuring passionate
secret admirers. Celebrate Valentine's Day with
these wonderfully romantic tales that are
ideally suited for this special time!

Available in February 1999 at your favorite retail outlet.

# HARLEQUIN®
*Makes any time special* ™

# Coming Next Month

### #2013 CONTRACT BABY Lynne Graham
### (The Husband Hunters)
Becoming a surrogate mother was Polly's only option when her mother needed a life-saving operation. But the baby's father was businessman Raul Zaforteza, and he would do anything to keep his unborn child—even marry Polly....

### #2014 THE MARRIAGE SURRENDER Michelle Reid
### (Presents Passion)
When Joanna had no choice but to turn to her estranged husband, Sandro, for help, he agreed, but on one condition: that she return to his bed—as his wife. But what would happen when he discovered her secret?

### #2015 THE BRIDE WORE SCARLET Diana Hamilton
When Daniel Faber met his stepbrother's mistress, Annie Kincaid, he decided the only way he could keep her away from his stepbrother was to kidnap her! But the plan had a fatal flaw—Daniel had realized he wanted Annie for himself!

### #2016 DANTE'S TWINS Catherine Spencer
### (Expecting!)
It wasn't just jealous colleagues who believed Leila was marrying for money; so did her boss, and fiancé Dante Rossi! How could Leila marry him without convincing him she was more than just the mother of his twins?

### #2017 ONE WEDDING REQUIRED! Sharon Kendrick
### (Wanted: One Wedding Dress)
Amber was delighted to be preparing to marry her boss, hunky Finn Fitzgerald. But after she gave an ill-advised interview to an unscrupulous journalist, it seemed there wasn't going to be a wedding at all....

### #2018 MISSION TO SEDUCE Sally Wentworth
Allie was certain she didn't need bodyguard Drake Marsden for her assignment in Russia. But Drake refused to leave her day or night, and then he decided that the safest place for her was in his bed!